Amelia Watchman

To All The CHEATS

ISBN: 978-1-913807-35-1

This story has taken a long time to finish and I'd like to dedicate this one to the Tamarillas team. They're not only always on hand to help me keep going, they are inspirational and strong women who I am lucky enough to call family. Thank you, Sophie, Mum and Barb.

To my husband, who is ever supportive and my beautiful girls who gave me plenty of stories for the two littlest characters in my book.

Other books by Amelia Watchman

It's all about me, maybe
All I want for Christmas ISN'T You
Love, Hate and Indifference

Children's:

There's a Dragon in my Garden

Chapter 1

'It'll be you and Will next, trust me.' Eloise squeezes my shoulder reassuringly and slinks over to the dressing table, perching herself on the mahogany seat. We've been in the bridal suite since last night, a short half hour drive from our home in Twinton but a far grander village nestled in the picturesque Cotswolds.

Eloise leans in close to examine her face in the mirror, gently brushing her fingertips over her spotless skin. There's really no need, she looks absolutely flawless, but then again, she always does. That's Eloise for you, if she wasn't so lovely, you'd have to hate her because she's so stunning that it's almost all that anyone can talk about. Even when we were children it was a *thing* and as she grew it became bigger and bigger. Not that I'm jealous or anything, of course.

'You really think so?' I can't help but smile as a tingly sensation ripples down my whole body. There were a few instances where I thought he might, but this time, I'm sure. My thirtieth is coming up this year, it's the perfect time. Will's been hinting at booking a holiday soon, especially after mooning over Eloise and Eddie's honeymoon plans, he was almost sulking he didn't get to go. Is there anything more romantic than proposing abroad, under the stars maybe, or watching a sunset, or dressed for the hot weather at a stunning restaurant. He's also been way more secretive recently, it's a sure sign that he has something planned. We've been together for over five years, it's the right time for the next step. I'm almost giddy, my hand starts to shake and I steady it, today isn't about me.

Eloise would be so pleased for us, but it's her day, her wedding day. She introduced me to Will, one of Eddie's, 'eligible bachelor friends'. She'd been determined to set me up and after a few non-starters, there he was. Will. Like a breath of fresh air, seemingly oblivious to Eloise's beauty and poise, it was impossible not to like him. Finally, someone who wasn't talking to me to get to her, or who couldn't hide the sideways glances. Someone who listened. Someone for me. Someone who felt the same.

'I do imagine us, a couple of wives together. It's going to be amazing.'

I rub at my cheeks as a wide grin spreads across my face, it's only the morning and we have a whole day of smiles to get through. Still, I imagine our shared lives; holidaying together as a foursome, dinner parties and eventually kids, perhaps we could even get pregnant at the same time, our children could grow up together, just like us.

Eloise stands up and brushes down her dress and I gasp. She looks like she's just stepped off the pages of *Vogue* magazine: bridal issue.

'You look beautiful. That dress is perfect, Eddie is going to love it.' The style wouldn't look right on many people, it wouldn't look right on me. Heavy on the lace, a sweetheart neckline and a slim fit that clings to every inch of her body, even an extra pound of fat would be revealed, luckily for Eloise she doesn't have any excess fat.

'Do you think so?' she asks shyly.

I nod, happy for my best friend. She's taking the next huge step in her life. We've been through so much together and now I get to be her maid of honour and, hopefully soon, she can be mine. It all feels so meant to be.

She spins around and I can hear the hairstylist squeal and clap in appreciation. This is the usual effect she has on people, I'm *almost* blind to it now but even I feel the tears pooling in my eyes. She's picture-perfect.

'Wow, you just look amazing,' the hairstylist gushes, snapping away with her camera phone, circling her like the paparazzi searching for the perfect shot. Her eyes widen. 'I think you might be one of the most beautiful brides I've ever seen, and I see *a lot.*'

'Aww thank you, I bet you say that to all the brides.' Eloise bats away her compliment coyly. The hairstylist shakes her head, and we all know that she doesn't.

She comes over to my hair now. 'So, what are we doing with your sister's hair?' she asks.

We both giggle; we've always been mistaken for sisters, we have a somewhat similar look, long blonde highlighted hair – we use the same hairdresser. Eloise found her, she's fabulous, normally she'd be here but she's off on her own honeymoon. Weddings really are in the air. Aside from the hair we both have greeny/blue eyes, although Eloise's are just a touch lighter and greener, and we have a similar build. But while Eloise's delicate features, big eyes and full lips create a gorgeously symmetrical face, I have an ever so slightly large nose and small, thin lips that don't lend quite the same effect, or so I've been told. *I* would be considered the ugly sister, the plain Jane or simply the other one. I think I've been called all those things in Eloise's presence at some point but it's not her fault that she was so blessed. In fact, she always gets so angry if people say anything like that, she says it's all nonsense, but she would because that's who she is.

'We've not sisters,' Eloise explains. 'I'm one of four, but all brothers, I'd have loved a sister growing up, although Anna is like a sister to me.' She grins broadly at me, she's the sibling I always longed for too.

The hairdresser looks startled. 'Don't worry it's a common mistake.' I raise my hand to stop her from continuing, turning my attention back to my hair. 'I'm having it up, is that right, Eloise?'

'Yes please, up for you to complement mine

being down.' Eloise has her blonde hair down with a soft curl that frames her face, a delicate veil placed strategically atop to finalise the look. I would much prefer mine down too, but I don't say anything. It's not my special day after all and I want her to be happy, she'd do the same for me. The hairstylist searches through her phone and finds the photo she took from the trial.

'Ah, yes,' she sighs. I peer at the image on the phone and I can't help but notice how the style seems to accentuate my nose, who knew that was possible?

'I love that dress on you.' Eloise's eyes alight on my canary yellow dress, it's full-length, cinched at the waist a little too tightly for my liking. I shouldn't have let them convince me to get the smaller size, I don't know how I'm going to fit the wedding breakfast in. Even the few sips of champagne I've had have left me feeling bloated.

'Yes,' the hairstylist agrees, barely looking at my dress and applying a bit too much enthusiasm. 'You look stunning too.'

I offer her a small smile, taking the afterthought.

'She does look so beautiful,' Eloise praises, making a fuss of me. 'Can you believe she wanted to wear something so much plainer, she can really pull off that colour. I wish you had more confidence in yourself.' She pops her hand on my arm, giving me a look, urging me to find more confidence in myself.

I give a tight smile and fiddle with my hands. I'm much more comfortable in more muted tones and this colour is not what I would normally wear but when we were choosing my dress with her mother, they both simply loved it.

The hairstylist nods along as she carefully curls my hair, lifting it up in places comparing it to her phone image.

'On second thoughts,' Eloise muses. 'She could have her hair half up, half down. Would you like that, Anna?' Her eyes search my face, looking for my approval.

'Are you sure? I'm happy with however you want it.' I keep my face neutral; I want her to have everything she wants today.

'I know you are because you're kind but I'm happy with however you want it,' she soothes, nudging me affectionately.

The corners of my mouth lift again, although she's not my sister, she can read my mind as though she were. 'I really don't mind, it's up to you.' I know it's already been decided, and I physically relax as the hairstylist sighs and softly pins up half of my hair.

When she's finished, I absolutely love my hair and the dress is growing on me. The hairstylist leaves and we're finally alone. I look over at Eloise who has suddenly gone quite pale, she sits down on the huge four poster bed that her and Eddie will share later tonight and begins to fan herself dramatically.

'Are you okay?' I ask, coming over and settling on the bed beside her.

Her glassy eyes rest on me and she nods along. 'Yes,' she says more sternly. 'Just feeling a bit nervous with everything. I can't believe it's my wedding day. It's *today*. It's finally here.'

'I know.' I pat her arm encouragingly, waiting for her to continue. A bit of wedding jitters is normal, I try to put myself in Eloise's shoes, this huge event in her life. A huge wedding like this, I know I'd feel overwhelmed. I'm surprised to see Eloise like this though, I thought she was practically unflappable. She stays unusually quiet.

'You'll feel better once you see Eddie, then everything will fall into place. Just focus on Eddie.' I keep my voice light, trying to reassure her, remind her what today is all about. She's been so composed all morning I'd assumed she would fly through this without the slightest wobble. It happens even to the best of us, it appears.

She offers me a watery smile. 'It's just a big day. I've been waiting for it my whole life and now it's here.'

It's a lot of pressure to put on one day. Everything has been organised to a tee. Eloise painstakingly designed everything she wanted in minute detail; the delicate hand-made place settings, the favours, bunting, special drinks named after the bride and groom in a cute and endearing way. No detail overlooked.

I go to my bag and pull out the bride and groom I've crocheted over the past month, careful not to squash them in my hands before I reveal them. There's no better time. Just us.

Eloise visibly brightens as I come back over to her, trying to peek at the obvious gift in my hands. 'What's that?'

I'm pleased she's momentarily distracted from

her wobble.

'I made something, silly, for you,' I say, popping them into her hands and feeling immediately embarrassed with all my work on show. Honestly, I'm pretty proud of them, they weren't easy to crochet and I started again several times but they turned out well in the end. 'This one is you and this one is Eddie.' I point out the detail and the colouring so she can see how they look like them.

'Wow, thank you, Anna. I didn't realise you still crocheted. I thought you gave up.' She examines the little figures, twisting and turning them in her hands. 'It's a funny sort of hobby for our age, isn't it? My aunt Agatha was into crocheting, or was it knitting?' she ponders aloud, but almost to herself.

I let my shoulders sag, slightly hurt. It's nothing new but it still stings. I've been crocheting since my nanny taught me when I was ten years old, back then I'd make endless friendship bracelet type things before I moved onto squares and blankets. Everyone always found the balls of yarn and crocheted cushion covers in my house amusing and I'm used to hearing the odd old lady comment. When I'd suggested to Will I was going to crochet them he'd thought I was silly and wasting my time but even he admitted they looked good when I'd finished. They're the first figures I've crocheted, normally sticking to blankets, hats, scarves and gloves but I thought the wedding warranted something special. Something personal.

Eloise looks over at me, sensing my disappointment. 'I love them, sorry Anna, they're absolutely wonderful. I suppose it's becoming more of a thing now. I saw someone with a crocheted dress that was so lovely. I only meant you're just so clever to be able to do this at such a young age. Thank you for this lovely gift, it's so thoughtful and must've taken so long.' She places them carefully on the bed and straightens up, a pinkish colour returning to her cheeks.

She composes herself. 'Could you do me a favour, Anna and check on the flowers and buttonholes for me please?'

There's the Eloise I know. Back to business, back in control.

I tidy the buttonholes counting them for the third time and making sure they're laid out ready to be pinned. There's a sharp tap at the door and Eloise's Dad enters the room; he's a tall and imposing man and the way he holds his chest always reminds me of a proud peacock. He's flanked by Will.

'Oh, what are you doing here?' I grin up at him, he looks around the room which looks like a bomb has hit it, clothes, makeup, and breakfast items in various stages of consumption strewn everywhere.

'Where's Eloise?' he asks as his eyes sweep over me. 'You look lovely, darling.' He drops a kiss onto my cheek awkwardly, his head swishing to and fro. He must know he shouldn't be here but I'm happy to see him regardless. He looks so handsome, and my quickening heartbeat reminds me this could be us. I imagine him standing at the altar waiting for me with pride in his eyes. We could have something smaller than this, something outside maybe; that would be so romantic. I sigh dreamily and Will clears his throat, drawing attention to me not answering his question, bringing me back into the room.

'Just finishing up getting ready.' I nod towards the bathroom. 'What are you doing here? Is everything okay with Eddie?' I bring myself back to reality, thinking the worst, Eddie wouldn't stand her up, he adores her. Will is the best man so if there is a message from Eddie, he would be the one to deliver it, a sense of dread takes over.

'Um, yes, he's fine, just thought I'd drop in and say hello.' He eyes the bathroom door before adding. 'Help Jeff out.' He gestures towards Eloise's Dad who's undoing all of my hard work fingering all of the buttonholes and picking out the best of the bunch for himself.

'Do you want to see Eloise before the wedding?' I watch him as he looks around, his eyes settling on the crocheted bride and groom on the bed. A small smirk flickers across his mouth for just a second.

'No, it's fine, I can see she's still getting ready. Eddie is feeling a bit nervous, wanted me to check she was still coming.' He chuckles to himself, bringing his eyes back to my face and giving me one of his devilish grins. 'Don't know what he's nervous about, I'm the one who has to give a speech.'

I laugh, feeling lighter. 'Sounds like the groom may still need you then. She's definitely coming I can assure you of that.' I try to usher him out of the room.

He nods curtly, getting the hint, then he plants another kiss on my cheek. He's in full tails, minus the top hat, and he looks truly gorgeous. He has a red waistcoat with gold trim on under the jacket. I take his hands reassuring him as he walks to the door, they're clammy. It's the last weekend in July and the summer sun has been out in full force all week; add the speech which he has been agonising over and it's no wonder he's a bit jittery. He lets out a long breath, peers again at the bathroom door and leaves.

Chapter 2

My bouquet of pink and red roses, with specs of green in the centres, complement my dress perfectly. I find myself constantly looking down at them as I walk, focusing in on the vibrant colours, concentrating on the scent. Even with the distraction, my knees are trembling. I try my hardest to appear steady and move slowly.

We must've practiced this a dozen times over the past few weeks, but it still feels like an eternity to me. The room is completely packed, no seat left unfilled, a sea of faces watching every painful step. Why did I agree to wear these stupid sandals? They're much too high. I try to walk normally but the throbbing has already begun and I've barely had them on an hour. I step on my dress and awkwardly tumble forward, catching myself and trying to remain composed. The photographer is snapping away at the front, I hope they didn't catch that. Poise, grace, emulate Eloise, I tell myself, trying to channel something that comes naturally to her, though not to me.

There are people I know from my childhood, some I look forward to speaking to later, friends from school, work colleagues and Eloise's brothers, straight backed, thick hair and similar in poise to Eloise. My own mum and dad plainly dressed and lurking in the background, like they did in my life, are right at the back. Mine and Eloise's lives have been so intertwined for so long it was only right they came, or so she said. They were delighted to receive her invitation; they've always thought she was wonderful. They would have loved to have a daughter like her.

I think my heart is almost ready to burst out of my chest when I finally reach the front. It wasn't my finest walk, but now it's done. A sigh of relief escapes from my lips, the worst part is over for me. Now I can just enjoy the day. Relax.

I search out Will's face, his presence calming. He stands at the front next to Eddie who's hopping from foot to foot and I remind myself to watch him when Eloise comes in, he already looks like he could burst into tears at any moment. A rim of sweat is collecting along his thick hairline. I lock eyes with Will and he mouths 'breathe,' the gesture and kindness helping to steady me. I turn and wait.

The sharp intake of breath is almost a collective sound as Eloise enters the room, clinging gently to Jeff. There are a few sneaky iPads and phones out to capture the moment. It's quite a sight to behold her against the backdrop of the grand country mansion, huge windows, patterned walls, the high, painted ceiling and still all eyes are drawn to her. She is a vision in white, the perfect bride, her hair cascading down her back and the white lace dress clinging in all the right places.

I turn to watch Eddie revelling in the special moment, imagining this to be a moment Eloise and I will talk about forever. Will is fiddling with his cravat, probably worrying about the speech again, I wish I could hold his hand, squeeze it and reassure him. I can't wait for his speech to be over so he can relax. Later we'll be dancing on the dance floor, laughing over his nerves. It's typical of him, he wants to do so well for his friend.

Eddie has tears streaming down his face now, there's never been any pretence with him, he is who he is, not too manly to cry. It's incredible to see his reaction, fresh tears spring to his eyes and he wipes gently at them as well as displaying his huge toothy grin. It's so big it looks painful, but he can't help himself. Eloise glides down the aisle, a serene smile on her face. She looks straight ahead to Eddie, there's no nervousness or tears from her, she looks strong and sure. She's ready.

I try to catch Will's eye so we can experience the love together, a shared message that this will be us one day too. He's staring straight ahead, too busy watching Eloise come down the aisle. Everyone is completely focused on Eloise and I can't blame them. This is truly her moment, well her and Eddie's moment. I'm so happy for them. My best friends.

'Good afternoon, everyone,' the officiant announces loudly, forcing the crowd to watch him. I take

Eloise's flowers with mine and stand at the front on Eloise's side. Will is over the aisle opposite me and I watch him. There's a tear in his deep brown eyes that I can't help but notice, I wonder if he'll cry when it's us? How will he propose? Is he already planning it? Eloise seems to think so; does she know something I don't know? It wouldn't surprise me if he confided in Eloise and Eddie. Eddie is his best friend after all.

I feel so full of love as I watch the looks between Eddie and Eloise. The officiant is a bit of a showman, if he wasn't an officiant, I wouldn't be surprised to see him on a West End stage. His voice is booming, and his arms move wildly around him as he enunciates each word, giving everything meaning.

'Eloise and Eddie have been together for ten years and have built a relationship of mutual trust, love and adoration. I'm told they met at university, Eddie, forever waiting around for Eloise to get ready but she was always worth the wait. Eddie, when asked to describe Eloise told me she's kind and clever, tenacious and sometimes pig-headed and always gets what she wants.' There's a collective laugh as we all agree with the assessment of Eloise. 'Eddie I'm told also possesses a pig-headedness.' Another laugh of agreement. 'A strong and fun-loving man who, we can all agree, has finally met his match.

'Today we take ourselves out of our usual daily routines to witness a unique moment in the lives of Eddie and Eloise. Today they join their lives in the union of marriage.' He gestures to Eloise and Eddie.

I look across at Will again, he's still listening intently, rigidly staring at the happy couple. I look down at his hands clasped together, his jaw clenched tight. The best man's job is clearly not an easy one. I've never seen him like this before, he's usually a real joker, light and fun. I resolve to get him a drink immediately after the ceremony, it'll help calm his nerves.

He's been very tight lipped about his speech, practising in private so I can't wait to hear it either. Poor thing, he's probably not even listening to the ceremony but running the words of his speech through his mind, ever the perfectionist. Public speaking doesn't come as easily to him as it does to Eddie but I have no doubt Will will do him proud.

'And so, it is that Eddie and Eloise present themselves to be married, surrounded by the people they love the most.' The officiant indicates around the room, involving us in the ceremony. Will clears his throat loudly, everyone turns their attention to him, and I see Eloise glare at him, her eyes widening.

'Sorry,' he croaks, everyone laughs, the tense atmosphere is broken.

The officiant clears his throat bringing the attention firmly back to where it should be, him.

'Eloise's mother, Shannon, is going to read a poem.'

I turn my attention to Shannon as she approaches the lectern. I glance at Will again, he's still focused on the floor, probably embarrassed about his badly timed cough. I turn, listening to the poem, a popular one for weddings but it's beautiful none the less.

'I carry your heart with me, I carry it in my heart…' Shannon starts, speaking beautifully, clearly. She really does Eloise proud; I beam up at her, encouraging her words. She's like a second mother to me, kind and graceful, Eloise is a lot like her.

As Shannon sits back down in the front row Will clears his throat again. I turn and collect my handbag from my seat, rooting around quietly to find the little bottle of water I put in there earlier, but I can't feel it anywhere. Having a tickle in your throat is the worst. Finally, Will clears his throat again and I look over as he stands. His hands are clasped in front of him and his face is red, although given the number of layers he has on it's no wonder. A single bead of sweat runs down his forehead and he looks almost in pain. His cough must be caught in his throat, perhaps he is going to go out the back to not disturb the ceremony. I look at him with pity in my eyes, he must be mortified.

'Ahem,' he starts, and eyes me. 'I'm sorry,' he murmurs, glancing at me for the first time since Eloise entered the room. Before I have a chance to contemplate what he's doing he coughs for a final time and loudly says, 'I object.'

Chapter 3

The officiant looks puzzled. It has to be a joke, it's not funny in the slightest but it has to be a joke. It's the only explanation. Eloise is going to have a shit fit at him later, come to think of it so am I. Is Eddie in on it? Although he looks confused and his neck is red and it's creeping up to his face. I search his eyes for the crinkle of laugher, ready for the joke to be revealed but it's clear, he's furious. He roughly wipes away the tears he shed when Eloise walked up the aisle.

'It's not funny, Will, sit down,' I hiss, thoroughly mortified by the whole thing, this cannot be real. My stomach churns; the sips of champagne we had this morning and the hastily eaten bagel swirling around.

Will thinks he's a real joker but his jokes aren't always funny. Even Eddie isn't laughing and he always laughs. This joke has not landed well. I just want him to sit down now so we can get on with the wedding and laugh about all of this later.

Will peers over at me again, his jaw is set in

determination and there's no smirk on his face. His dark brown eyes are filled with tears.

'I'm sorry, Anna. I mean it,' he says, and a single tear runs down his face as he turns and looks at Eloise, adoration in his eyes. 'I love Eloise. I object,' he says firmly, nodding again, his gaze not shifting from Eloise's face. Eloise stands bewildered in the midst of this.

There's a collective gasp from the entire room and whispered murmurs hover like a hive of buzzing bees. Whispers of, 'What did he say?' reach me from the back and the wind is knocked out of me as I try to take in what's happening. Everything is loud and the room is spinning. I don't know what to do, so I do what I always do. I look to Eloise, my best friend, for answers.

She's now staring at the carpet as though it's the most interesting design she's ever seen, refusing to meet anyone's eyes. The girl with so much to say has not a word. Eddie is trying to get her to speak, but she seems to have lost her voice. She's gone so deathly white; against Eddie's furious red face they look quite the pair. The officiant leaps into action, not missing a beat.

'Hold on folks we're just going to pop out for a quick chat and then we'll be right back. Chat amongst yourselves.' And with that he mutters, 'Follow me,' to Eloise, Eddie and Will. Although he says it quietly you can hear the disgust in his tone.

He turns without another word and the four of us, because this involves me, shuffle after him like school children being led to the head teacher's office. We enter a side room which is mainly used for the music and is underwhelming by comparison to the rest of the place.

I'm trying to understand what just happened. I don't know where to stand, is this the end of us? Has something been going on? I don't believe Eloise would do that though. Eddie is pacing backwards and forwards at speed, if he continues, he'll wear right through the carpet. He's no longer red but puce, ready to explode. Eloise is still this meek version of herself, looking anywhere but up.

'What the fuck mate? You're in love with Eloise? My fiancée, my about to be wife?' Eddie roars. 'And this is the time to tell me?'

'Yes.' Will's conviction is cutting; the world around me starts to spin again. This is real. This is happening. It's not a joke. The officiant takes a tentative step forward trying to put some space between Eddie and Will.

'Well, I've never had anyone object before,' he ponders loudly. 'We don't even ask if anyone objects. What do you want to do?' The officiant waits for someone to tell him.

Eddie isn't listening, he's not focused on the officiant's words. 'Is something going on between the two of you?' Eddie asks, his pain is palpable as he scrutinises Eloise, searching for the answers. Surely not. Eloise loves Eddie, they've been planning this wedding for over a year. When would she have had time for an affair with *my* boyfriend?

Eloise doesn't say anything, she looks between me and Eddie, her mouth forming little o's as she does so. I can't believe it. I look down at my flowers and my horrible dress, which appears to be getting tighter and tighter as this continues. I'm still holding Eloise's flowers too. I drop them to the floor not caring where they land.

'Tell them, or I will.' Will's voice is harsh and filled with venom.

I look at him; who is this man?

Finally, Eloise's voice returns. 'Yes,' she whimpers, bringing her hands up to her face and weeping loudly. 'I'm..ss…sooo….s..s..orry.'

After that there's a ringing in my head so loud that I feel the need to scream and shout but I hold it in. My hand flies up to my mouth as I feel my stomach contents begin to brim. I turn on my heels. I run.

'Anna, wait,' Eloise calls. 'I can explain.'

But I don't want to hear it, what possible explanation is there?

I run back through the grand room stopping briefly to pick up my handbag. I can hear whispers and talking but I don't focus on any of it, I keep my eyes focused on the door ready for my escape.

How can this be? Eloise and Will? Will and Eloise? I toss their names around in my head, but it doesn't matter which way I cut it; it doesn't make sense.

The doors are heavy, and I push and push at them, the tears have already begun pouring down my face and I let out a frustrated. 'Argghh'. I'm aware of everyone watching me but I keep my focus, this door will open. Then I will be free.

Suddenly the door swings open and I fall through,

another gasp from the crowds, it's like being in a bloody pantomime. Oh no she didn't. Oh yes, she fucking did and apparently with my boyfriend. I look to the side to see my parents standing close by, they must've helped with the door but I didn't even notice.

I ignore them, not wanting to speak, and run down the stairs and out into the open where I bend over breathing deeply, savouring the fresh air, pleased it's not the hottest part of the day yet.

'Oh Anna.' My mum comes over to rub my back but I'm not ready to compute what's just happened. I don't want to discuss it. I put my hand up to stop her or to shield me, I don't know which.

'Do you want us to take you home?' my dad ventures, his voice soft and low.

My head's swirling around and around. Home? I can't imagine going back to the home I've shared with Will for the past five years. Where is my home now?

I shake my head and as I do the rest of the wedding guests begin to spill out into the grounds. I can hear mumbling and chatting becoming louder and louder. There's even some laughter. What is there to laugh about right now? I see some of my friends making a beeline for me and I suddenly feel the need to be really far away, alone. I swipe away the tears from my face and busy myself rummaging through my handbag, finding my keys. We brought Will's car with us, a sporty number that is his pride and joy. We're not far from home but we came up yesterday, I stayed in the suite with Eloise and Will had drinks in the bar with Eddie before staying in what would be our room for tonight. I re-focus on the car, I hate driving it but it's all I have. It'll have to do.

Mum and Dad watch me with concern, their mouths bobbing open and closed with questions as they try to decide how to speak to me. They've never been great at that. What is there to say when a mansion full of people have watched your humiliation?

I straighten up, trying to compose myself. I don't want everyone to see me break down.

'I'm going to go,' I say with more conviction than I feel.

'Good idea,' Dad agrees, starting to walk alongside me. Mum steps closer awkwardly, normally this would be the part where a mother would embrace a child but not mine, that's not who she is.

'No, sorry. I meant alone.' I wipe away another flurry of tears and set my jaw; my mind won't be changed.

'Anna, I really think you should come with us. You've had a nasty shock,' Mum begins to protest. 'Is there something going on between Will and Eloise?' she asks, her voice is disbelieving, and I don't know the answers to begin to discuss it with her. I bet they're more disappointed than I am; they've always loved Eloise and Will, probably more than me.

'I'll be fine,' I say through gritted teeth. Ignoring her questions about Will.

'Okay well we're going to go home, come round anytime. You have your key,' Dad says, taking Mum by the arm and ushering her towards their car.

I break into a run, rushing over to Will's car and jamming the keys in the lock, I'm not even being careful. Will would have a fit and the vision of scratching the key along the side of the deep green car makes me almost want to smile, but I don't do it.

I get in the car and drive quickly out of the car park, thankful I'm not blocked in.

I don't look back.

Chapter 4

The first time, when I was young, I didn't understand. A boy holding my hand one day, the next, another's. Teddy. It's not a big thing, he's not worth it, you'll make other friends, you could do better. He loved my hair, it was a real thing for a six-year-old, all the way down to my bum, a soft golden brown, not dyed blonde like now, but it was beautiful. But then she came, a white-blonde, hair just a fraction longer and he was gone. Gently stroking *her* hair beside me, what's the problem, he's only six? But it still hurt my feelings, there were things unsaid and so it began.

Fast forward to being an awkward fifteen-year-old. He was my first real boyfriend, Jared, with the boyfriend label and everything. First kiss, first awkward fumble, first one to say I love you. We spent every week at the local ice rink skating rings around each other and falling more and more in love. Or so I thought. He went with his friends and I went with mine, a regular teenage hangout.

Everything was good until I caught him snogging another girl beside the lockers. It was over. I was heartbroken. Weeks went on. He wasn't worth it, I needed to dry my eyes, I could do so much better anyway. He paraded girl after girl at the ice rink. I stopped going.

Dating here and there nothing went anywhere until at twenty I met Derek. A romantic, aspiring poet (although he was rubbish, even I could see that). He was sweet and sensitive, perhaps a little too sensitive. It wasn't his fault, she preyed on him. That's what he said, the poor guy didn't stand a chance. Tricked by a regular Venus flytrap. It was only once, it didn't mean anything, he was drunk, his friends egged him on. Ever the victim. I couldn't even look at him, it was over.

Finally, at twenty-four I met Will, through Eloise of course, so ironic now. Give him a chance, she said. He's different, you'll like him. He's a proper gentleman and he's funny, good looking in a non-conventional way she said. No pressure, just a quick dinner, the four of us. I didn't hold out much hope because this was the third of Eloise's set ups and the others had been more enamoured with Eloise than bothered with speaking to me. Not this time. With Will sparks flew, Eloise had got it right with Will. He'd never cheated on any of his previous girlfriends. I thought he was the one. A proper gent. The end of my story.

I press my foot down on the accelerator; the tears that I held in streaming down my face. I've missed the turning towards home, I can't bear the thought of walking into our memories, I'm not ready to face it all. The soft top is open and my eyes water even more from the blast of wind in my face. Now I wish my hair was all pinned up, but only half is pinned to within an inch of its life and the rest flies around my face and gathers in my mouth, as my thoughts whirl around all my past relationships and failures.

I've been on the motorway for a while, having driven past our turn off what feels like ages ago. The venue was only a short drive from our home but it felt wrong to go there, not that I know where I'm headed but the need to go fast has never been so strong. I decide to pull over at the next stop, because I need to get out of these clothes. This dress is cutting me in half now. I remember Eloise when we were choosing my dress persuading me to have the tighter one; I could lose a few pounds and it would be perfect. Well, I didn't. Some of us aren't perfect like Eloise, she lost nearly a stone even though she didn't have an extra ounce of fat on her in the first place. I wince just thinking about her. How long has it been going on? How could he? How could she? It doesn't make any sense. My breathing begins to quicken and I indicate hard to go into the services. The tears are flowing fast now, I can barely see, this isn't safe. I try to steady my breathing, just five minutes and I can get out the car.

Breathe. Breathe. Breathe. I turn into the car park and pull into the first space I see. There's a family just pulling up next to me and I get out of the car ignoring their curious glances. I double over and try to breathe in deeply but the dress is restricting me. I can't breathe. I pull at the dress to try and loosen it but it's no use. My panic starts to build and I claw at the dress until finally it begins to give. I breathe deeply, finally free of my dress and becoming more and more aware of my surroundings.

I look over to see the family in their car gawping at me, the mum's hands covering a little boy's eyes. I look down to see that in my haste to free myself from the dress, I've pulled it really far down and my disgusting beige bra is on full display. From a distance it may even look as though I'm topless. Excellent. I pull my dress over myself holding it to me and try to apologise profusely to the family. I see the dad's amused expression, but the mum looks furious.

I ignore them and head to the car boot. Perhaps I can find something in the boot to cover myself with.

I wish I'd thought this through a little bit more and grabbed some clothes before I left but the shock hadn't allowed for rational thinking. I can't keep wearing the dress now there's a huge rip down the back.

I rummage around in his boot and my hand lands upon a duffle bag. Bingo, hopefully this'll have a coat or something I can cover myself up with and reduce others' attention. The bag is obviously one of Will's gym bags, clearly forgotten because the clothes smell fusty with sweat and damp. There's a hint of Will's favourite aftershave which brings a fresh wave of nausea and makes me incredibly sad. I pop the t-shirt on pulling it on over my dress, trying to press the feelings down and concentrate on the task in hand. The shirt falls down to mid-thigh just a little too short to wear alone but I can't keep the dress on a second longer. I pull the dress off underneath trying to maintain my dignity as I go.

I hear another tut-tut as the woman from the car next to me marches past, her little boy in tow. He can't be more than six years old; he's laughing as he passes and hanging off her arm. Great. I fish around in the bag and pull out some cycle shorts, fab. Something I didn't like about Will is his need to wear these. I throw them on, they're really tight and it takes some wiggling to get them on but they cover the last of my dignity. Damn you, Will. There are no shoes that fit me and so I still have my stupid high strappy sandals on.

I head into the services, it looks pretty big, with any luck I'll be able to get something else to wear.

Fortunately, in the weird collection of shops there happens to be a section selling holiday clothes. Swimming costumes, towels and a tie-dyed hooded towel which is the closest thing I'm going to get to an outfit. I take it over to the till along with a pair of flip flops that my feet are throbbing to put on, together with a packet of gum and wet wipes to clean up, what I don't doubt is, a mess of a face.

I head off to the bathroom and begin the process of unpinning my hair. There are so many pins in the top it hurts, as it comes down it's kinked and messy, a perfect bird's nest. I really could do with a brush but I don't want to go back to the shop. I just want to leave.

My makeup is everywhere, mascara tracks under each eye, smeared lipstick, there's even some on my teeth, was that there earlier? I begin the process of cleaning; it's a lot more make up than I'm used to wearing and I find myself really scrubbing at it, taking my frustration out on my poor face.

'Oh dear, are you okay?' A concerned looking lady with big hair and double denim asks whilst I clean the black streaks off my face.

'I'm fine. Just a bad day.' I feign a smile, suddenly desperate to get out of here, the tears threatening to fall again.

'We all have those sometimes.' She smiles back at me offering me a small chocolate bar from her bag.

'I couldn't.' I shake my head at her.

'You can,' she says and balances it on the sink next to mine. I could almost cry; the kindness of strangers. In amongst my whole life falling apart this lady who doesn't know me cares.

I glance at the chocolate but leave it there, I'll pick it up when I'm done. 'Thank you,' I say, as she leaves.

As I continue the assault on my face the harassed looking woman and her son come out of one of the cubicles, the boy runs straight to the sink and to the chocolate bar. Grabbing it he hides it in his pocket. His mum sees what he's done. He isn't fast enough to pull one over on her.

'What've you got there?' she asks, eyeing *me* suspiciously, a soft tone to her voice as she addresses him.

'Nothing, Mummy.' He smiles sweetly, but he's

not an accomplished liar and his constant fidgeting gives him away.

'You have something, what is it? Give it to me.' She puts her hand out and her tone has hardened; a tired and unimpressed edge to it. I keep my eyes forward even though the commotion is going on right beside me, is almost about me, if I look, I'll have to participate and I don't think this lady is my biggest fan.

'No, Mummy it's mine, she gave it to me.' He pops his bottom lip out in a pout, changing his voice to the whingey one he undoubtedly uses when he's tries to get his own way.

'Who gave it to you?' she asks angrily.

The little boy thrusts his podgy finger towards me. 'She did,' he says. 'The woman without any nibbles.'

'I didn't give him any nibbles, he took my chocolate,' I explain to the woman as she narrows her eyes at me, not believing me for a second.

'You did,' the little boy insists. 'And you're weird. You have no nibbles, just like my sister's Barbie.' He scrunches up his nose and points to my chest which sets off a flashback of my ugly beige bra in the carpark.

Chapter 5

After an awkward standoff with the woman where it was ascertained that I did not try to steal her child or give him anything poisoned (seriously?) the little boy makes off with my pity chocolate and I'm left at the sink in relative peace again.

I pull my newly bought tie-dyed hooded towel on and take off the top that smells of Will. I shove it in the bin along with my uncomfortable sandals without a moment of regret and think about how, effectively, that's what Will has done to me. I wonder if he had a moment of regret. Are he and Eloise eloping now? I shake my head trying to remove the thoughts of them rushing around in my mind, but instead I find myself exploring every memory for a sign. I was blind to it all. There was nothing there, or so I thought.

Perhaps I should have stayed at the wedding and faced it all. I made my decision; I choose flight not fight and now I've stopped for a second, I don't know what I'm doing or where I'm going. I glance at myself in the full-length mirror helpfully installed on the entire wall as you leave the toilets, seems necessary as everyone looks their best when travelling, not.

The tears seep from my eyes again; I take some deep breaths to steady myself. It's okay. It's okay I tell myself but it's not, I look ridiculous. My hair is a knotty, wild mess and my face is red raw from all the scrubbing. The outfit is not my best and I still have the tags hanging from the side. I tug at them pulling at the plastic that's determined not to budge from the towel until finally it gives way creating a small hole in the corner. Great. That sums up my day. Even with the towel thing covering everything from the front I keep Will's stinking shorts on as the sides are open.

I can't face the thought of going home to my parents, all the pitying looks and fussing over everything that's happened. No, I don't want that right now. My mother's constant hovering and Dad's cooking and since they stopped working all the cleaning up after me would be just too much. One time I was mid-bite when Dad started taking my plate to wash it up, it's obsessive. How I longed for them to be around more when I was a child but now, I'd prefer to be left home alone for hours.

I decide, given my current get up, to head to the coast and I feel instantly brighter at the thought of being even further away from the disaster that is my life. I can practically smell the sea air and the fish and chips. Perhaps it's the tie-dyed towel talking but the idea of feeling the cool sand between my toes has never been so appealing. I head back onto the motorway and about five minutes in I wonder if I've made a huge mistake. There are tailbacks on both sides. I suppose this is what a nice day in July does. Sends everyone to the beach.

After almost four hours on what would normally be a two-hour drive, I arrive at the beach. The drive was gruelling, and I don't fancy driving back anytime soon. I go straight onto the sand and pull off my new flip flops. Ah, that feels good. The beach is packed, there are kids screaming and running around. I walk down to the sea front and put my feet into the sea, it's freezing cold but it's a welcome distraction. There's a blissful anonymity to being here all alone whilst the families and couples all around me sunbathe, play and swim. They're not interested in me; they don't know my world has fallen apart. I'm just a woman with slightly crazy hair and questionable dress sense. At least my outfit isn't such a strange choice here, although I am a little hot and wish I had something cooler to wear. Perhaps I should have bought a swimming costume.

I sit down in a quieter, shaded spot and pull out my mobile, there are loads of missed calls from an array of people, some of them from people I've hardly spoken to in recent months. School friends who were at the wedding who got to witness my humiliation first-hand. There's also a spattering of calls from Eloise and Will, the cheek of them. There are some messages and voicemails but I decide not to read or listen to them. What can anyone say to make it better? Everyone wants the scoop; I am a hot commodity now.

I see a few calls from Mum and Dad and so I text Mum to let her know I'm fine and I'll call her in a few days when my head is cleared, and she need not worry. She pings a message straight back saying she was so worried, and I try to reassure her again before switching my phone off. I don't want other voices in my head right now. I put my hand to my face and realise the tears are falling again. I wipe at them trying to refocus on where I am, forget about what happened. I watch the surfers try to catch the waves and the kids running, I focus on the here and now and not on the what's happened.

I sit for a while, a low growl from my stomach reminds me I'm famished. I've not eaten all day aside from the meagre amount I had whilst we were getting ready, it seems so long ago now, I can hardly believe it's the same day. I find a little chippy to the side of the beach and fill myself up with the most delicious fish and chips before heading back to the sand. The sun begins to set and I decide I better find somewhere to sleep. I can't face the drive back now. I need to sleep for three years or until everything is over.

The yearning for a comfortable bed and privacy is unbearable. There are a number of Bed & Breakfast places along the promenade and so I head over to them. They'll be expensive but there's never been a time where I need it more. I try not to overthink the money aspect, to stop myself unpicking mine and Will's expenses.

The first B&B I get to is beautifully painted,

whites and blues with a huge wooden anchor at the front. There's some nice seating in the garden, which is well maintained, and it looks gorgeous against the sea backdrop. I head in and there's a teenage boy on reception.

'Mummmm!' he shouts. 'Customer.' He puts his head back down, his greasy hair flopping over his face, consumed once more by his phone. His job complete.

A plump, middle-aged, brown-haired woman who's clearly "mum" comes into the room.

'Sorry about him.' She inclines her head towards the teenage boy who makes no effort to look up or even acknowledge her. 'Can't get the staff,' she says and there's a playful manner in her words. 'How can I help you dear?'

I smile politely. 'I was wondering if you had a room available, please?'

She baulks at me for a moment and then recovers. 'Oh dear, have you not booked?' she asks, her voice friendly but concerned for me.

'Um, no. It wasn't exactly a planned trip.'

'I see, I see.' She nods along looking through her books. 'I'm afraid we don't have anything. It's the summer holidays you know, we're booked solid. It's a very popular place and with the weather being forecast as so nice I don't think you'll find anywhere. You could try Molly's, it's a few streets back that way.' She indicates with her podgy fingers further away from the coast.

'Okay, it's okay. I should have been more prepared, I'll try Molly's.' I say to placate the woman, her carefully plucked eyebrows drawing into the middle. Her warm, friendly face could make me crack at any moment, she only needs to ask if I'm okay, so I hurry out of the place as the woman and her teenage son gawp at the idiot who hasn't thought to book anything in advance.

Molly's is kitsch and not as well looked after as the first B&B, the paint is peeling and the garden is slightly overgrown and it could all do with a good tidy. I persevere, I need somewhere to sleep, my standards have definitely dropped, hopefully so will the expense. My feet are aching now and it's starting to get dark, I don't fancy walking around for much longer. When I get inside a round faced man, who is presumably not Molly, is in the hallway.

'Do you have a room available?' I rush, my voice lifting up at the end in slight panic.

Not-Molly laughs for a full minute before he shakes his head. 'Sorry love, I just thought you were kidding for a moment. We're booked solid, did you not see the forecast?' he asks gruffly, his voice low and gravelly.

Yes, I knew the forecast, Eloise had been watching the weather like a hawk all week, with regular updates on what the temperature would be on her special day.

I hang my head down, saddened by my decisions and try to think what I'm going to do now. I just don't want to drive home. I sigh loudly and I bite my lip to stop it from wobbling.

'Look I can try the hotel round the corner for you?' he offers, a kinder tone to his voice.

I nod solemnly, I can't take much more today.

Not-Molly spends some time on the phone, mumbling and grunting and laughing and finally pops the phone down.

'Sorry love, there's really nothing. My mate there was saying the whole town's probably booked out. Have you travelled far?' he asks in a soft voice, appraising me with his eyes and settling his stare onto my hair.

'Um yes, no. It's fine,' I mumble, as I try to walk out of the B&B and get as far away as possible.

'Wait love,' he yells as I turn to walk away. 'I shouldn't be telling you this but there's a little layby over the way towards Duckpond Farm, you can park up and sleep in your car there. You might have better luck in the morning with the hotels.'

I nod my head, looks like it's a night in the car then.

I head back to the beach and enjoy watching the water in the moonlight. Suddenly I become very aware of being all alone on the sands and I decide it's time. I drive over to Duckpond Farm which takes some finding, the hood's still down on the car and although it's been warm all day it is chilly now. I need to work out how to put the hood up. I never really paid much attention. It was always Will's job, Will's car, he would barely let me drive it let alone put the hood up. His fancy sports car against my boring *Micra*.

I park up in what I assume is the layby Not-Molly was talking about and try to figure out the buttons. What do I press? I feel exposed to the elements and a bit scared. I'm on a country road in a scary layby with the top down, the last light is almost gone. Anything could happen. The clouds have moved in and there's an ominous feeling. I sit back and breathe deeply. There's only one thing for it. I'm going to have to drive home but as if to stop me the heavens open, the rain is strong and driving right across me. I'm soaked in minutes. I can't see anything let alone drive and I know it wouldn't be safe to leave now. I scream out loud. Could this day get any worse? I scream and shout into the rain, it feels almost therapeutic as the low guttural sound erupts from my body. I jab desperately at the dashboard and finally, after what feels like an eternity and a thorough soaking, the hood mechanism starts to work, bringing itself down into position.

Finally sheltered from the elements, I turn the heaters on and try to get warm. There's nothing in the car and it's pretty late now. I take my soaked tie dye towel off; it's not doing anything to help but at least it stopped my cycling shorts from getting wet. I sit there in my beige bra and cycling shorts and it feels like the perfect end to the worst day. I pull the seat back and try to sleep.

Chapter 6

Tap tap tap.

What's that noise? A groan escapes from within me and I try to ignore the sound.

Tap tap tap.

I open my eyes and it's still dark and I'm cold. So cold. How did I even fall asleep? Last thing I remember is sitting shivering in the car, trying my hardest not to think about Eloise or Will. I close my eyes again.

Tap tap tap.

Focus, focus. What's that noise? I'm awake now. I turn my head to see some eyes peering into the steamed-up car. I doubt they can really see me. Oh my God is this how I get murdered? Here in this little layby? perhaps Not-Molly isn't as innocent and friendly as he seemed and he lured me here. I've been so stupid; this is a classic beginning of a horror film. The panic rises in my chest as I think of my foolishness and picture Mum and Dad sobbing over my body. If they find it, that is. Maybe I'll be missing for years, or he'll take me to an underground bunker where I'll live until I'm found or escape ten years later. Would they let Will attend my funeral? They better not, or Eloise for that matter, I don't need her crocodile tears. This is all their fault.

I press the button down to lock the car and pray they'll go away. If I don't look at him it'll be okay, perhaps he'll give up. I try to turn the engine on, feeling the puddle of water underfoot that formed when I tried, and failed, to close the soft top. It's stopped raining now, typical. The car won't start; did I leave something on when I fell asleep?

There's another tap, tap, tap along with a voice this time.

'Excuse me, excuse me.' It sounds like a woman and I instantly feel safer, I just hope she's not here to traffic me somewhere. I smear away a little of the condensation with my hand so I can see her.

She's your typical old lady, small, with grey wiry permed hair, half-moon glasses. She's dressed for the wilds and as she peers further into the car I almost laugh with relief. I don't think she's going to murder or traffic me anywhere.

'We're not into dogging around here, young lady.' Her strong Cornish accent comes through and she sounds less than impressed. 'Move along or I'll call the police.' Her voice is stern and angry, it makes me think of my nanny, I hated being told off by Nanny.

'Um, no I'm not dogging.' I recoil at saying the word dogging to this sweet looking old lady.

'I can't hear you; you're going to have to roll the window down,' she shouts, tapping at the car again.

I pull up the lock and open the door a crack. A small gush of water dribbles from the car and she lets out a small gasp as she watches it flow over her boots.

'Okay dear, what's going on here then because you've hardly got any clothes on in there. Is there a man in there? Has somebody hurt you?' She pulls herself as close to the car as possible and tries to look in through the inch of opened door.

And like that the tears spring to my eyes as I experience the humiliation of the wedding all over again. Will. Eloise. Driving to the coast. Nowhere to stay.

'Hello?' The old lady is losing her patience now but I can't answer her because I'm too busy trying to hold it all together. 'Dear, do you need me to get someone? Have you broken down?' she asks, concern filling her eyes and it's too much, her angry face changing to that of a soft granny has done it.

The fountain of tears begins to fall. I'm sobbing and sobbing, there are no words, I just nod feebly trying to calm my jerking body.

'Oh dear! It can't be that bad surely, why don't you come down to the house with me and have a cup of tea. You look like you need it. I've probably got some clothes that'll fit you.'

I nod again, not able to get words out and pull my wet hooded towel back on, it's still sopping wet and now carries the smell of damp.

I step out of the car, wondering what the time is. It's dark now. My body is shaking from head to toe, the cold chilling me to the bone.

'I must say, you weren't what I expected to get out of the car. You look like you normally sleep in a tent not a sports car…' The old lady uses a walking stick but she moves fast and sure.

I look down at myself; she's right, I look like some kind of weird hippy. I try to compose myself. 'You were the last person I expected to see in the middle of the night,' I counter.

'Middle of the night? It's barely ten-thirty, dear. I was just walking back from the pub and I saw you parked in my layby.' She motions into the distance with her cane.

'Oh, well thank you.'

'Quite. Now let's get in and get you dry, you look frozen. Can't have someone dying in my layby, wouldn't be good for business.' She grins at me and I can't help but smile back for the first time in hours.

Her house must have been part of a working farm at one point, but I can see it's not any longer. She fusses at the doorway taking off her boots and her thin raincoat. She's wearing a grey-brown, longish tweed skirt and white shirt on underneath which makes her look like an old-school headteacher.

'Now come through, come through.' She leads me to the kitchen, gesturing at where I should sit. It's a beautiful farmhouse kitchen with a huge wooden table in the middle. She goes over to the stove and sticks the kettle on. There are lots of knick-knacks around and photos of various people. The room is beautiful and cosy, although there's a light coating of dust on everything, making the house look even older.

She disappears into one of the other rooms and comes back with a towel and some clothing.

'It's not as fashionable as what you're currently wearing but it'll do.' She says the word fashionable with a certain amount of distaste which implies she believes what I'm wearing to be anything but fashionable and beyond her understanding. 'The bathroom is at the top of the stairs to the left. Best to wait until the morning for a shower, there's no hot water now.' She points up the stairs and I head out to go and get changed. I look at the outfit and it's a full-length, white nightdress.

I dry myself off and change, glad to get out of my cold, wet clothes. Feeling and looking like a 1920s ghost, I head back downstairs to find a mug of what looks like builder's tea on the table. I take a tentative sip and it tastes sweet, there's clearly at least two spoonsful of sugar in there too. I've always been a bit of an extra milk, no sugar type of girl. The little old lady comes back into the room.

'Thank you,' I say. 'For everything. I'm Anna by the way.' Feeling utterly mortified and imposing, what am I doing?

'I'm Dorothy,' she says, studying me. 'Friends call me Dotty. You can call me Dotty.' Her tone has softened, perhaps me not dressed as a hippy in a soft top sports car has helped.

'So, Anna, what were you doing in my layby?' She raises her eyebrows.

And just like that, I find myself telling Dotty the whole sorry tale of how I got here.

Chapter 7

'I think it might be tricky to get that car fixed around here. I know Dale down at the garage, want me to speak to him for you?' Dotty has taken pity on me and allowed me to stay the night.

I really need to work out what I'm going to do now.

'Yes, thank you,' I mumble.

I'm sitting at the table with Dotty, she's fully dressed but I'm still attired in her long, flowy nightdress. It might not be much to look at but in fairness it's incredibly comfortable. When Dotty offered for me to stay the night it started me off on another round of sobbing, so it wasn't until the very early hours that we got to sleep. Dotty was so kind and sympathetic, she didn't judge, but offered helpful insights into mine and Will's relationship.

Now it's back to reality. My head hurts as I think about the car and what to do with it, the memory of the puddle in the footwell brings a weird satisfaction to me, Will won't be pleased. Good.

'I've popped your clothes in the tumble dryer, they should be done soon. I still don't understand what kids wear these days.' She shrugs as she plonks another builder's tea in front of me.

She doesn't ask me how much sugar or milk I want, it's the exact same cup of tea every time and I have to admit something about it tastes pretty good, although it's still a little sweet. I'd normally overthink something like this and only allow myself one on a bad day, a pick me up. I suppose yesterday counts as a month's worth of bad days, so I take a big sip and resolve not to allow my mind to run away with itself. I'd also never dream of making a cup of tea without knowing how someone likes it but this doesn't bother Dotty.

I think of Eloise's cup, watery, milky, no sugar; and Wills, strong, one sugar, splash of milk.

'I better pop out and fetch the eggs. I won't be long; would you like some eggs for breakfast?' Dotty asks, pulling me back into the room. She scurries around the kitchen, fetching a small basket from the counter.

'Um, no I'm okay. I don't want to impose. I should really get back.' I'm acutely aware I've cried all over this poor woman who probably wants nothing more than for me to leave. A new sense of awkwardness engulfs me.

'Don't be silly, they're fresh. I'll just do you two and we'll see how you get on. No need to hurry home on my account, you're welcome with me.' She fetches her stick from the big kitchen cupboard and heads out of the door. 'Feel free to take a shower whilst I'm gone, fresh towels in the airing cupboard.'

She doesn't need to tell me twice. I head straight to the shower. The water running over my face and body feels heavenly, it begins to reinvigorate me and I find myself singing "I'm going to wash that man right out of my hair", so apt right now. This is the best I've felt since before it all happened and I'm pleased with the distraction.

I step out of the shower and that's when I realise, I didn't get a towel out of the airing cupboard. I peek out of the bathroom; Dotty must still be outside with the chickens so I'm sure it'll be fine. She doesn't move fast and I kept the shower short, not wanting to take advantage of Dotty's hospitality. I see a couple of doors near the end of the hallway, one of them must be the airing cupboard, it's really not that far. I can pop down there and get one. I pad lightly hoping not to get Dotty's attention if she is in the house, although I doubt she'd move fast enough to see me. Halfway down the hallway I hear the front door slam and some mumbled voices. I run down the hallway and pull the door open but it's not the airing cupboard. I'm starring into what is presumably Dotty's bedroom.

Then the screaming begins.

'Daddy! Daddy!' I spin round to see a little girl, who can't be more than five years old, staring at me like I'm crazy.

'There's a nakey lady who's trying to take Granny's things,' she wails at the top of her lungs.

I stand there startled, trying to cover myself. She turns back to me. 'Are you trying to steal some clothes, nakey lady?' she whispers, in a conspiratorial tone.

In my haste to get away before whoever she's with comes up the stairs, I step into Dotty's bedroom and pull the door closed.

'Daddy, Daddy, she's hiding in Granny's room.'

'What's going on up here then? What are you shouting about, Hazel?' a low, male voice asks.

'What Hazel shouting bout Dada?' says a little voice, the words are spread out. She repeats the phrase a few more times in exactly the same sing-song way.

'She's hiding in there.' Hazel presumably points at my location and I hold the door handle tight. Now what?

'Granny's in there?' the low, smooth voice asks.

'No Daddy.' The little girl sounds exasperated, there's a little 'No Daddy,' parroted from the smaller voice. 'Nakey lady's in there.'

'What's in there?' her daddy asks, a gentleness in his voice.

'A nakey lady of course.'

'You have some imagination, Hazel.' He laughs, a big booming heartfelt laugh. Confident and friendly.

'No Uncy Joe, she's in there. I promise, ask Santa, I'm not lying.' She sounds stroppy.

I can imagine her bottom lip out in irritation. I resolve to keep silent, perhaps if they don't believe her, I think guiltily, they'll all go back downstairs.

The laughter stops and I suddenly feel the door handle rattle as I desperately try to hold on for dear life but whoever's pulling the door is stronger than I am and the door begins to move.

'Hmm, something appears to be holding the door or it's stuck.'

'I'm naked,' bursts from my mouth as a shrill shout and the handle stops pulling. I open the door just a crack so they can see my eyes, positioning my body behind the door and saving my modesty.

I see four pairs of eyes staring back, two men, two children.

'Who are you?' asks a man with dark wavy hair and blue eyes, his eyebrows pulled into a frown and a very serious expression on this face. There's the first little girl, presumably Hazel and another even littler girl, perhaps two-ish with tiny blonde curls and a cheeky face. Hazel has her arms crossed.

'Told you there was a nakey lady, Daddy,' she says triumphantly.

Another man with a huge smirk and similar eyes but thick blonde hair stands to his side. They're clearly brothers but the blonde man has a lightness to his face which makes him appear happier than his sterner brother who does not appear to find anything funny in this situation.

'Who that, Dada? Who that, Dada?' the girl with curls asks, tugging impatiently on her daddy's hand.

'Who is that, Daddy?' Hazel joins in, putting her hands on her hips and staring hard at me. Attitude and sass in abundance.

I feel like the big bad wolf. God I'm glad I wasn't still dressed in Granny's clothes, although, that would have been better than how I'm currently dressed.

'I was taking a shower and I forgot to get a towel from the airing cupboard.' I stumble over my words but surely, they'll all see it's an easy mistake to make, even if I do sound ridiculous.

'Um okay,' the little girl's Daddy begins, but as he goes to speak again, he's interrupted.

'That is my guest,' Dotty's voice booms, putting them all in their place, her headteacher persona coming out in full force. 'You lot should come downstairs and let her get dressed. I'll put some eggs on for you all.' She turns her attention to me, a smile playing on her lips. 'The towels are in the bathroom dear, in the airing cupboard. I'll pop your clothes in there on the way,' she mutters.

'I'll just wait up here for our guest,' the blonde smirks, leaning against the banister.

'No, you will not, you rascal, come downstairs.' Dotty swats at him indulgently.

'Naughty Uncy Joe, got told off by Granny,' laughs Hazel.

'Naught-eee Unc-eee Joe.' Repeats the blonde curls, screwing up her face to Uncle Joe. He lifts up the little girl and she squeals with delight as he carries her back down the stairs.

I nip back into the bathroom and notice the small cupboard in the corner and shake my head at my foolishness.

I wonder how long the men and the little girls will be here and whether I can stay up in the bathroom until they've left. *That* was mortifying.

Chapter 8

As I come downstairs, I hear the buzz of voices before I enter the room. There's laughter and a constant stream of chatter coming from two little voices, getting louder and louder as they both try to speak over each other. It's not something I'm used to; my parents weren't cruel but distant, we rarely ate meals together growing up. I was an only child and they both worked long hours. My parents were both only children too, so no aunts, no uncles, how I longed for a big family when I was younger. Just Grandma and Grandpa, Mum and Dad that was it.

I often wondered if I was a mistake, but it doesn't seem like that here. They are here to visit Granny, they want to be together, they're not a burden. I close my eyes and try to stop the tears from coming, thinking of how I spent so much time at Eloise's house, her family was the family I always wanted, there was fun, laughter, siblings and a lot of time spent together and now they're all gone. I can't face them. Eloise has taken them from me as well as Will.

She's taken it all.

'Oh, there you are dear.'

I look uncomfortably down at my outfit, the cycling shorts and psychedelic hooded towel that are so not me but are the only clothes I currently have. My hand unconsciously touches my wet hair and I'm very aware of my raw, make-up free face, scrubbed clean and bright red. The lack of makeup makes me feel self-conscious. I by no means cake it on but I always have the basics; foundation, blusher, a lipstick and mascara. My face of armour for the day because you've got to make the best of what you have, that's what Eloise is always saying. What do I care though? I don't know these people. I attempt a smile, baring my teeth which probably looks more like a grimace but the little girls beam back anyway and suddenly my smile isn't so forced.

'I was just telling the boys about you.' Dotty nods towards the two men, who are certainly not boys.

With beautiful square jawlines and thick heads of hair, the 'boys' watch me. I wince; do they know my humiliation? Would Dotty have told them the whole sorry affair? A fresh flush creeps up my neck. I can't escape it, not even here. Why did I tell Dotty?

'Anna, these are my grandsons; Joe.' She gestures to the blonde hunk, his hair is slightly longer, which lends itself to a certain surfer vibe. 'Max.' She nods over to the serious brunette, his frown giving him a brooding quality, reminiscent of Mr Darcy. They both have the same piercing blue eyes. 'And these two little mischief makers are Hazel and Neve.'

'Nene,' says the little blonde girl, her ringlets

bouncing around as she gets down from the table and spins around dancing. 'Nene.' There's a collective aww and laugh as Neve dances, enjoying her own name. With a lot of effort and refusal to be helped by anyone she climbs back up onto the seat.

'She calls herself Nene,' Hazel informs me, in a very matter of a fact voice. 'It's her nickname, I don't have a nickname, I'm just Hazel. Although sometimes Daddy calls me Pumpkin, but I am *not* a pumpkin.' She growls the last bit looking at the man who's just been introduced as Max. The words coming out in a rush of excitement.

'Hello, I'm Anna and I don't have a nickname either,' I say awkwardly, feeling like I'm intruding on a lovely family morning. It's like something out of a family sitcom, very wholesome, they're just missing the freshly baked muffins and orange juice.

'I totally forgot to tell the boys you were coming. Silly me and my memory.' Dotty makes a show of hitting her head and looking pointedly at me. I nod along mutely.

'Hmm, yes,' Max clears his throat. 'Gran tells us you're a carer.' He gives me a stern look. '*Interesting* outfits they wear these days.' The distaste for my outfit is clear in the delivery of his words.

'Oh, shut up,' Dotty says, but there's a gleam of mischief in her eyes and I can't help but think of her making a similar observation only yesterday, although I don't think Dotty's delivery came across as quite so rude. 'She can wear whatever she likes if she's staying here as well as looking after me. I was telling them, dear, about how you're a live-in nurse-carer.' She eyes me cautiously, nodding pleadingly at me. 'This lot thought I'd found you at the end of the road or something.' She forces a laugh which lands a little flatly. 'They're always telling me off for bringing home strays. They say it's dangerous, but I've told them it's not like that this time.'

'We've been trying to convince her to get a live-in for so long, we're really pleased to have someone,' Joe explains. There's a little twinkle in his eye which makes me feel hot and bothered.

I stop myself from touching my cheeks, no need to draw attention to my less than perfect face. I don't know the first thing about being a carer but if Dotty needs me to pretend that's what I am, I will, especially considering everything she has done for me. And it's much better than the sorry reason I am here. I suddenly feel grateful to Dotty, instead of embarrassing me, she's lied to her family to protect me.

'I could have helped with this though, Gran. I told you I know a girl who works in carer recruitment.' As Max says this, he eyes me suspiciously. 'How *did* Gran find you?' He directs his question at me, but it's more of an accusation than a question.

'It's been handled, I used an agency. Why do you need the ins and outs? She's here now like you wanted, we don't need to dwell on it,' says Dotty, taking control of the situation again and I find myself wondering what I've signed up for here.

'Yes, what does it matter, bro?' Joe asks, patting Max on the back. 'Gran's sorted it.' He casts a big cheeky smile towards Dotty who matches his grin back, are they in cahoots, does Joe know?

'Thank you, Joe, I'm more than capable.' Her voice is stern and Max opens his mouth as if to argue and then closes it again, clearly thinking better of it.

'We'll discuss this later,' he finally agrees, turning his attention back to his breakfast and the girls. 'Eat up girls we've got some errands to run.' He busies himself scraping the food around his plate.

'Oh Daddy, I don't want to run boooor-ing errands,' Hazel whines.

'Boring errands,' repeats Neve, screwing up her little face to imitate her sister.

'You can leave them here with us for a few hours if you need to,' Dotty offers, as Max's gaze rests on me again.

I busy myself eating my eggs, not long now and I'll be on my way out of here, if I can work out how to get the car fixed. Dotty can explain the carer stuff away, whatever that's about, perhaps she'll say it didn't work out or something.

'Joe, are you staying for a bit?' Dotty asks.

'Can do, Gran,' he says, but he twinkles at me again and I find myself blushing back at him, despite my whole world falling apart, despite my best friend betraying me with my boyfriend, I find myself smiling at him and I let myself enjoy it. 'Will you be joining us, Anna?'

'Umm, umm' I stammer. I really should get the car sorted.

'Course she will, that's the point, isn't it?' Max harumphs, looking at me accusingly, daring me to argue.

I guess I am.

Dotty casts a weary look in my direction and I decide to go along with it. She did put me up overnight after all and she's fed me and looked after me, it's the least I can do. I couldn't head home even if I wanted to until the car is fixed.

'Yes,' I say with more conviction than I feel.

'We'll go down to the beach, what do you think?' she asks, whilst Nene climbs down from her chair and begins a dance whilst shouting 'dance' at the top of her lungs.

I could go to the beach with them for a few hours and then sort the car out, no big deal. It's not like I'm in a rush to get back home anyway. Nothing there for me now.

'Yes, sounds good,' I say, breezily.

The morning at the beach is the best I've had in ages. I immerse myself in this other life, running around with the children, in and out of the sea, simultaneously trying to catch the waves and run away from them. Their giggles and pure joy at the beach fills me with such warmth. Joe's the doting uncle running after them, becoming the wave monster and playing silly games. His company is like a breath of fresh air and I can't help but watch his athletic body as he moves around so fluidly. We spend several hours building the biggest sandcastle. Neve eats a fair amount of sand and Hazel meticulously designs how the sandcastle should look, fighting with Neve and telling us off when we stray from the very specific plans she's made.

After a while I go and sit up on the beach with Dotty.

She gives me an apprehensive look, her soft grey hair blowing gently in the wind, before turning her attention back to the children, her eyes lighting up and her face glowing as she watches them run around. Her pride and joy.

'I'm sorry I've landed you in it, I hope you don't mind just pretending to be my carer whilst they're down. It'll keep them off my back for a bit,' she says, sheepishly.

'Why are they so determined that you need a carer; you seem very capable to me.' I think back to Dotty finding me last night, yes, she may walk with a cane, occasionally, but she seems fully able to me.

'Oh, you know, family.' She shrugs like it says it all, but I don't really know. 'They worry,' she expands. 'They're based in London through the week, and they come down most weekends. It's silly really, I'll probably outlive them all. My own mum lived to be one-hundred-and-one; you know.'

'Wow.' My eyes drift back to Joe running up and down the beach. I try to focus my attention back on Neve and Hazel flattening and jumping on sandcastles, but I can't stop being drawn back to him. He's broader than Will and probably a little shorter too, and he's certainly more handsome. He's good-looking in a very obvious way, a heartthrob way and I remind myself that he probably has a whole harem of girlfriends back in London and I'm not getting into that. But a girl can look right? He's a nice distraction from Will.

I try to mentally shake Will out of my head, because whenever I think of Will I begin to think of Will and Eloise and then everything begins to spin and I think I might break. My eyes begin to well and I try to refocus on the girls and Joe, this glorious man just before me. I'd imagined children with Will, we'd be married first and not long after we'd have our first, twins perhaps and then I could be done all at once but now I'm starting all over again. No ring, no wedding, no kids. Not Will's anyway. I mourn the life we could have had.

'You alright dear?' Dotty's voice cuts across my thoughts, pulling me out of the rabbit hole I'm circling.

'Yes, I'm fine,' I say, but an involuntary tear trickles down my face, betraying me. I swipe it away roughly, embarrassed.

'Why don't you stay for a while? You could be my pretend carer, get the boys off my back and perhaps get some space from everything going on back home? Could be a solution for both of us? Besides, even with my connections they won't even look at the car until tomorrow, never mind fix it.'

I put my hands into the sand, relishing the feel of it between my fingers. Thinking about what to do. I don't want to go home; I can't bear the thought of going back to the cold house I grew up in. I've lost my home, my partner, my best friend and future all at once.

'What have you got to lose?' she asks, already sensing I'm convinced.

Nothing at all.

Chapter 9

We walk back to Dotty's house and I mull over her words. Staying feels like the best thing to do right now. I suppose I'll need to get in touch with work but I'm sure it'll be fine. Most of my colleagues witnessed my shame first-hand so I doubt anyone could deny or would be surprised by me taking a few weeks off. With a sense of foreboding, I picture them all asking about the wedding, Will, where I went afterwards and why.

I don't know what Eloise and Will have told everyone but regardless the shame of how it looks fills the pit of my stomach. I stop myself going down that rabbit hole, I'm owed leave anyway. I'd been saving it for a holiday with Will later in the year. My proposal holiday. I take a deep breath.

Maybe the job is something else I'll have to lose.

I'm front of house at the local hotel; Eloise helped me get the job. She helped me with everything really. She's the general manager now, with her degree in hospitality and tourism management making her the perfect candidate. She was the deputy manager when I first started and oversaw my work a lot more back then; I'm just pleased I don't report to her anymore. I don't see her that much at work really, she's off doing all the paperwork in the back office and presumably in between lunches, which she often took with me, having an affair with my boyfriend.

She's off for the next month on her extended honeymoon. A once in a lifetime trip, Eddie had been so excited about it, they'd planned it meticulously together, a travelling month-long honeymoon extravaganza. We'd all had a good laugh about that together, I'd mooned over it with Eloise for weeks, noting all the places I would suggest Will and I take ours. Los Angeles, San Francisco, Las Vegas, before relaxing in the Caribbean for the last week. No expense spared.

I wonder if she's taking that honeymoon, and who with? She has her pick of the bunch now.

'You alright?' Joe asks, falling into step with me. He gives me a big grin showing me his perfect, straight teeth. I bet he never even needed an orthodontist. Not like me, I wince thinking of my crooked bunny teeth. Thank God for braces.

'Yes, fine.' I try to turn the corners of my mouth up, but it's strained, fake.

He gives me a puzzled look but chooses not to comment, pulling his hand through his hair instead.

'Are you new to the area? I feel like I'd recognise you if you came from here?' His eyes continue to search my face and I wonder if I'm about to be found out. I'm a fake. He knows. I'm no carer. It's all a lie.

'Do you know everyone from this area?' I deflect. He's probably dated all the women from around here.

'Well, I thought I did.' He chuckles at his own joke, his whole face lighting up as he laughs.

I don't reply, preferring to walk quietly back. Watching the girls skip around Dotty while she guides them out of her way.

He narrows his eyes at me, really exploring my face. 'I grew up around here, it's not a huge town. Where are you from?'

'Bit more inland,' I reply, noncommittally. I don't want to discuss our backgrounds or where we grew up or who we were. Or any of it. Invariably all roads lead back to Eloise, and then Will and I just want to evict them from my head. I imagine them as a piece of torn newspaper, screwing them up and throwing them away, but they're still there, hovering.

'You're a mysterious lady. Thank you for looking after Gran, she's amazing. I'm glad she has someone to be down here with her more,' he says, pulling his fingers through his luscious locks. I try my hardest to keep from falling at his feet, this man, he could make me forget. There's something about him that's so easy to be around and him being a doting grandson and uncle certainly helps.

'Anyway, sorry about my brother. He can be a real stick in the mud.' He rolls his eyes as he describes the brooding brunette.

I think back to Max's accusing eyes. Surely, I can

pull off being a carer for a few weeks; I need to go out and get some fresh clothes but then I can hang out with a lovely old lady and put off dealing with all my problems for a little while.

'It's fine, he was just being a good grandson. This isn't how I'd normally dress.' I indicate my clothing and I wonder why I feel the need to explain anything to this handsome stranger. This could be how I dress. What's wrong with it?

Joe doesn't comment on my attire. 'Would you perhaps like to go out for lunch or dinner or something?' His voice is sure and confident and I can tell he's asked this question many times before.

'Oh um, I don't know, maybe. I'm your Gran's carer…' I trail off grasping at straws because it's hard to say no to his lovely face but I'm not ready to be dating, if this is a date?

'No worries.' He shrugs. There's no argument and I'm almost disappointed that he doesn't fight harder, but it doesn't matter. I'm not ready to date anyone and certainly not someone like him, he's sure to be a womaniser with a face like that.

He smirks at me and I could almost change my mind but I hold steady, no I will not date the first lothario I encounter.

'We should exchange numbers though,' he says. As I start to protest, he stops me. 'In case you need me for Gran of course.' He widens his eyes, the picture of innocence. 'It's nice to have friends, especially if you don't know anyone around here.'

I'm slightly irritated by his presumptions but I pull out my phone and turn it on. It pings again and again with voice and WhatsApp messages. I could almost laugh, now who needs friends?

'Woah, you're popular, too busy for dinner.'

I swipe the messages away and exchange numbers with Joe and then switch the phone off. I'll deal with all of them later. Not now.

'Okay, I'll stay,' I say to Dotty.

Dotty's busying herself making her signature tea, gliding around her kitchen effortlessly in a type of dance. Does she really need a carer? Max collected the girls in a hurry, barely looking in my direction but being sure to ask if I had any references he could follow up. Dotty fortunately squashed that, with a tut she said she'd done it all properly herself and he was to stop treating her like an imbecile. I have the distinct impression that Max isn't that fussed on me, but that's fine. I'm not too fussed on him either. Joe headed back with him to London, and I'd be lying to myself not to admit I was kind of disappointed. Just a few hours in his company had made me feel a tiny bit lighter and it was nice to have someone good to look at.

'That's great, I am pleased. It'll do you a world of good. The sea air and sand are very healing you know.'

'Of course, I can help you out too,' I rush, thinking about the boys and who they think I really am. I don't want to take advantage of Dotty's kindness. 'I can pay you too, for my keep.'

'Contrary to my grandson's belief I am perfectly fine and capable on my own and I'm not needing any money and I won't accept it from you,' Dotty stands tall as she speaks, bringing herself up to her full height which would come up to my shoulders if I stood up. I stay seated at the table and nod. I fiddle with my teacup. I've been told and in no uncertain terms.

'Of course, but if you need anything, don't hesitate to ask.' I dither, an air of awkwardness suddenly falling over us.

'No problem, and ignore Max. Sometimes I wish he'd take a leaf out of Joe's book. He's always made friends so easily.'

'I bet he does.' It slips out before I realise and I pop my hand over my mouth. 'As you know I'm not looking for anything like that,' I say trying to backtrack, but my cheeks begin to burn hot, betraying me.

'No, I know. You're not Joe's usual type anyway, but a friend might do you some good.'

I mull over not being Joe's type in my head and I can't help but find myself feeling irritated. I'm not his usual type; too frumpy? Too old? Too ugly? Why am I not his usual type? What's wrong with me? Not Eloise. I bet she'd be his type. She's everyone's type.

I turn my phone on and tap out a text message to Jane, my manager, and am relieved that I no longer report to Eloise. Should I leave my job? I can't even imagine looking at her now but what else could I do?

Message to Jane
Hi Jane, I'm sure you saw what happened at the wedding. I've

got a load of leave I was saving for a holiday. I'd like to take two weeks now. I'll be in touch to sort out coming back into work soon. Hope that's okay and you understand? Anna x

I send a second message to my mum, typing quickly, keen to turn my phone off in case Jane says no. Then what?

Message to Mum
Don't worry about me, I'm fine, I'm staying with a friend on the coast and I'm going to take some holiday for a few weeks, clear my head. I'll be in touch when I can. Anna x

As I go to turn the phone off, I see a message from Joe and I chide myself for my reaction. My heart skips a beat. What is happening to me? It's just some displaced feelings from everything that's going on.

Message to Anna
Hi Anna, was lovely to meet you today. Lunch or dinner next Saturday? Joe x

Not his usual type. I find myself typing back to accept. Maybe Dotty's right and I could do with a friend. A handsome friend would certainly help.

Chapter 10

The next morning, I get up and out early. Dotty's doing some work in the house and cleaning out the chickens which I offer to help with, but she refuses. Ever the independent lady, she's right she'll probably outlive us all.

I catch the bus into town following Dotty's instructions and adore perusing the little high street. The shops are your typical expensive surfer type shops with a few charity shops interspersed, they're more expensive than I remember charity shops being but the clothes are also much nicer so I go with it. Now isn't the time to punish myself for spending. Retail therapy is definitely a thing and I need it.

Maybe it's something about wearing the psychedelic colours for the past few days that makes me purchase some beautiful dresses, skirts and cardigans in more vivid colours. They're far away from the more practical, neutral clothes I usually wear but I love them. I go to town buying practically a whole new wardrobe, enjoying it being my choice. I've never really thought about it before but I always shopped with Eloise and I guess I'd kind of adopted her style, albeit a more muted version. I looked to Eloise for opinions and approvals. Without her here I realise how intertwined our lives really were, I miss my friend and I hate her all the more for that.

My new clothes all have a beachy feel. What would it be like to live in these wonderful surroundings and stay here? I can't imagine why Joe or Max ever moved away. It's hard to be unhappy here, even for someone who is heartbroken, like me.

I pop into the local *Boots* which is a quarter of the size of the one near me and get myself some lippy and BB cream to stop myself from looking like death. Finally, I pop to the hairdressers and am delighted when they can fit me in immediately. Much to the hairdresser's disappointment, I opt for a more natural colour, turning my hair back to the mousey brown it really is and a shorter cut. I watch myself in the mirror, it's almost therapeutic, getting Eloise out of my hair, setting myself free of Will.

Will. I wince at the memory of him standing up, declaring his love for Eloise. How much of a fool have I been not to notice? Why was I so blind to it all? What did I do to make Will go off with Eloise? I try to push the thoughts away. No point in dwelling.

When I get back to the house Dotty is sitting at the kitchen table. There's a smell of something baking in the oven and the worktops look freshly wiped.

'I've just made a pot, fancy a tea?'

'Please.' I smile and she looks down pointedly at my many shopping bags.

'I figured some new clothes were in order.' A flash of red rises on my face at my overindulgence. I'll probably regret all of these purchases in the morning. What was I thinking? Can I really pull them off?

'Quite.' Dotty grins conspiratorially, nodding her approval. 'Nothing like a bit of retail therapy and I love the new hair, it suits you much better. Why don't you go and throw some of those clothes on and we'll pop down to the local pub for lunch? My cake's almost done and we can head back after for that once it's cooled.'

'Sounds amazing,' I say, and I take a big gulp of my tea and head upstairs to change.

I pick a beautiful floaty dress, it's so comfortable, the colours are gorgeous and I feel fantastic. I spend some time looking in the mirror, applying my new subtle makeup and letting my dress swish around my ankles. I love the baby blue colour, it really does make my eyes pop, especially with my hair. I enjoy the soft waves around my face. I've always kept my hair straight or curled, never wearing my natural waves but they look so lovely I don't know why I didn't do it sooner. The hairdresser encouraged me to embrace my natural wave, and look at me. I couldn't look less like Eloise and it makes me smile. I head downstairs.

'Wow, you look lovely. I much prefer it to the towel dress. I hope you don't mind me saying.'

'Not at all.' I laugh. 'I prefer it too.' I'm wearing more clothes but I feel lighter.

As we enter the pub it's clear Dotty knows everyone in here. They smile and wave and she greets everyone with warmth and kindness. She's clearly a very loved lady and I can see why. Taking in strays, she almost feels like *my* Granny now and in the short time I've known her I've become very fond of her and her no-nonsense nature.

'Have you lived here all your life?' I ask Dotty, wondering more about Dotty's life and how she ended up on an old farm in the middle of nowhere. She's clearly a social butterfly.

'No, not me. I'm from a large town about ten miles from here.'

I shake my head. 'So how did you end up here?'

'Tale as old as time, fell in love, didn't I. He was the man of my dreams.'

'It was his farm?' I try to imagine Dotty's home as a working farm. Dotty's not afraid of getting her hands dirty so I'm sure a young Dotty embraced the challenge.

'Oh yes, it was in the family for years, we ran it for a while but it just couldn't make enough money, in the end we sold off some of the land, kept a fair bit mind and lived happily ever after. Well, until he had a massive heart attack that is.'

'Oh,' I mutter at my insensitivity, unsure what to say. 'I'm sorry for your loss.'

'It's okay dear, was a long time ago.' There's a smile in her eyes and I can see she's back with her love, reminiscing over their shared past.

'How old was he when he died?' I ask, unsure if it's appropriate.

'Only forty-seven. Unfortunately, Max and Joe never knew him. He was a wonderful man. He was very kind and he had these huge hands. He was always making something. He had a way with furniture, he made the kitchen table you know? That was his real passion, not working on the farm and if he'd lived longer who knows what he would have achieved and that is why you should live however you like to. It doesn't matter what others think. Even grandsons who think they know best.' She winks at me, a cheeky glint in her eyes and I see the soul of a much younger woman, a woman who would probably have been very pretty in her day and not wanting for suiters.

'You never remarried?' I ask. Suddenly realising the rudeness of my question, I put my hands to my mouth.

This makes Dotty hoot with laughter. 'Oh, don't mind me, ask whatever you like. There's no secrets here. No, never met anyone that compared to Joe, and yes my grandson is named after him. My daughter really loved her father.'

'That's just lovely. Where is Joe and Max's mother?' I grit my teeth as I ask hoping not to hear another tragedy in this sweet family.

'She lives abroad, she'll be over later in the year to see everyone of course. She couldn't have named Joe better, there's definitely something about Joe that is just like his grandad, although young Joe lives more of a bachelor lifestyle. He just needs to find someone good enough to change his mind.' She grins at me and I can't help but wonder if she's hinting at something.

Does she think I'm someone good, but she said I wasn't his type?

'What are your plans for the week?' Dotty asks, changing the subject and I shrug, I don't really have any plans. 'Why don't you go out and learn to surf or dive or anything really, there's lots of options here and lots of fun to be had.'

I nod along but I don't really know what to do with myself. I suppose I've not really given it much thought. I kind of always went along with Eloise, she went to university after school, I didn't but we remained close. I had a few jobs in clothes shops, coffee shops and then when Eloise was settling into her role at the hotel after university, she helped me, I thought it was a good fit. I thought I was happy with everything.

There's only ever been one hobby that was completely mine and that was crocheting. I feel sick thinking about the crochet figures I laboured over for weeks while Eloise and Will were off laughing at me behind my back. No, I can't do that, don't even go there.

'Maybe I'll try and do some cooking,' I venture, thinking of the aromas from the kitchen earlier, and the cake cooling on the rack ready for our return.

'Oh, are you a good cook?' Dotty studies me.

I think over the few times I cooked for Will and shake my head. We normally had a food order kit come in every week that would provide all the ingredients and instructions and we'd do that. No thought processes needed.

'Um, I'm not really sure.' It strikes me I don't really know what I'm good at.

'You'll figure it all out. Make the most of being down here while you can. It's a magical place to live.'

I nod along, excited at the prospect of trying something new.

Over the week I try my hand at cooking which I'm actually really bad at. After a batch of salty biscuits Dotty removes my cooking privileges and endeavours to make the most delicious fruit cake. My dreams of becoming the next baking sensation disappear. Clearly, I'm not about to open up a bakery down here and live out my days along the coast. I fill much of the week down at the beach and reading which I enjoy enormously. I can't remember the last time I spent this amount of time immersed in a good book. One day, after finishing my book, I spot a sign for paddle boarding. It doesn't look as hard core as surfing or diving but it looks fun so I decide to give it a go and book myself a lesson.

I head over to the reception desk at the surf shop. The guy in there is your typical surfer type, longish, bright blonde hair, slim but muscular physic and a lovely golden tan you can even see through his light shirt.

'I'd like to book a paddle boarding lesson,' I say, with more confidence than I feel.

'Excellent, we can do that. I'm Teddy by the way.' He runs his hand through his luscious hair.

As he says his name, I find myself squinting at him. He has a bit of a Cornish twang but there's something awfully familiar about him. Teddy, I've not heard that name in a long time. He's taller, older, more slimline, his hair longer than it was but his eyes are the same dark shade of brown.

'Are you from round here, Teddy?' I venture.

'I'm from Twinton. And you?'

'Teddy Huddle?'

He nods his head and as he does his eyes search mine, does he recognise me too? I certainly haven't forgotten him.

'I'm Anna Robinson. We went to primary school together.'

'Anna,' he smiles but his eyes betray him. He doesn't remember me. I can see it.

'Do you remember me?' I ask. We were inseparable for a while, how can he not?

'I had long, long brown hair.' I use my hand to portray the full length. And like that his eyes light up and he says my name again but this time with meaning.

'I can fit you in for a paddle board in about an hour if you fancy it?'

'Yes sure,' I say, letting him off the hook, watching him brush his hand through his hair again, remembering when he used to do that to mine. I walk back out.

Teddy Huddle. What are the chances?

Chapter 11

I head back to see Teddy; over the last half hour my nerves have got the better of me and I've popped to the loo three times. I don't know what I'm more nervous about, the paddle boarding or spending time with Teddy. It's weird, I know barely anything about him now, but I remember him back then and how hurt I was when he chose another girl. I remind myself we were only young, that I can't hold this against him but a burning rage is beginning to simmer all the same. I need to get a grip. I can't pigeonhole him into the same box as Will, he was six years old.

Maybe Will was like this at a young age too, continuing having affairs here and there. Too clever to get caught. I never even caught him, he outed himself or I'd never have known. He could have carried on, married me and I'd have been none the wiser. The bile begins to rise in my throat again, is there enough time for another trip to the toilet? I could have married him and never known.

I push the door open and search out Teddy, he's standing next to the life jackets, leaning against one of the walls. He has an ease about him, there's no hurry, no worries. He belongs here on the white sandy beaches, catching waves, all surfer dude and high fives. He probably has five women on the go at once. It's all in a day's work.

'Right let's get you sorted, shall we?' he begins.

I try to mentally pretend he's just some random guy but my mind is running on overdrive, playing out different scenarios. Six-year-old me confronting Teddy, standing up for myself for once, but that's not how it played out.

'Right let's head out onto the sand and I'll talk you through the basics, then we'll go out onto the water for a paddle around. It's really not too difficult. I'm sure you'll be fine at it.' He offers me a pearly white-toothed grin and I want to punch him.

'Okay, sure,' I say, through gritted teeth. Cheat.

I shake off my anger, focusing instead on the task at hand. Teddy goes through how to use the paddle in the water, hand placement, how to stand – feet shoulder width apart, knees slightly bent. How to get on the board and finally how to get up to standing. We do this part in really shallow waters and I seem to be doing it okay. I'm totally immersed in what we're doing, it will be fine. Teddy *can* be my instructor. He shows me how to turn and we're ready to head out.

'We're going to paddle around the coast a little, up over to those caves and then we'll head back in.

That should be plenty for a first session. If you want to book any more sessions after you can let me know or if you're feeling confident you may even be able to head out alone. For some that can be after a few sessions though, depending on your capabilities and confidence.'

I nod meekly, I can do this. Maybe I'll be really good at it, a natural.

'You can start off on your knees for a little bit if you like, until you feel more comfortable and then stand up.' He goes through the motions again of what I need to do.

'Um okay,' I say, getting into a kneeling position on the board in the water. I begin paddling and it feels wonderful. I'm actually doing it. I'm elated.

'You're doing pretty well,' Teddy enthuses, a thumbs up thrown my way. 'Why don't you try standing up?'

And before I know it, I'm up on the board. I steady myself as the upward trajectory rocks the board. I'm up. I take a deep breath, breathe and paddle, breathe and paddle. I'm doing it. I feel great. Exhilarated.

'Once you get used to it it's pretty easy to stay on. You're looking good, Anna.'

A huge grin spreads across my face.

He smiles at me and those teeth bring it back again, gone is the elation of the moment replaced by a hot fury rising in my chest. My mind is buzzing. He doesn't have the right to smile at me, not when he went off to twirl someone else's hair. My God I'm going crazy; I remind myself that was a long time ago. Let it go. Why is this even bothering me so much?

'You okay there?' Teddy asks, soft lines across his forehead. 'You've got a really weird look on your face.'

'I'm fine.' I set my jaw and concentrate on making my face seem neutral. If only he was someone else, why Teddy? Thrash, thrash, thrash on the water. I really give it some with my paddle, perhaps if I put some distance between us, it'll feel a bit better. After all, maybe I *am* a natural.

'You sure?' he asks, unconvinced. 'Now you want to start to turn so you don't head too close to the coastline. Come a bit closer to me. There's a huge tree branch ahead.'

I begin to try to turn the paddleboard, using the paddle, to and fro like Teddy showed me to turn.

'Anna, Anna!' I suddenly hear Teddy calling my name.

I look up away from the paddle. I'm no closer to Teddy than I was a few minutes ago.

'YOU. ARE. PADDLING. THE. WRONG. WAY,' he shouts loudly and slowly.

I shift my focus back just in time to see I'm headed right into the hanging tree. I thrash about with the paddle; it only seems to move me closer until it's all happening too fast. I've lost control. I thrash with the paddle this way and that, but nothing is working. Whack. I'm off the board and kicking around in the water.

I kick and splutter, unsure which way is up and then suddenly I'm being pulled. My head breaks the water and I'm thrashing around wildly. There's Teddy, calm. Even while I'm drowning there is an ease to his being, there's no hurry. He does this all the time. He pulls me up and helps me onto my board, I lie on it, spread out, panting at the sky.

'Wow, you got completely wiped out there. I've never seen anyone ride a paddleboard into a tree before.' There's a laugh in his voice that infuriates me. I continue to pant, concentrating on my breathing as the anger surges again.

'It's not funny,' I whimper, and before I know it there are tears.

'Oh, come on now,' his tone is gentle, caring, but I'm not having it. 'You're okay you just had a little scare. Do you think you can paddle back or should I help you? Perhaps you could just stay on your knees.'

'Do you think you cannot cheat on people?' I spit it out like venom and it startles Teddy. He's probably not used to this tone in his airy-fairy life, all no worries and high fives.

'Umm I'm not cheating on anybody.' He looks puzzled and has slightly lost his easy, breezy edge.

'Yeah, right,' I mumble and continue to lie on the board. Breathe in and out. In and out.

'Just kick your legs and we'll be back on the shoreline in no time.' He's giving up on me paddleboarding back. An analogy for how he gave up on me for another.

Once we're back on the shore I stretch out on the beach, closing my eyes to prevent the tears from coming and zone into the warmth of the sun on my face.

'Are you okay?' Teddy asks, grounding me. I'd almost forgotten he was there. He runs his fingers through his hair, his signature move.

'Um yes.' I feel slightly embarrassed about my over-the-top outburst and before I know it, I find myself reminiscing about when we were together. 'I know we were young but you were my sort of boyfriend and then you were gone and I never said anything,' I try to explain but even to my own ears it sounds ludicrous.

I can hear there's a smile in his voice when he speaks. 'That was a very long time ago.'

'I know,' I appease. I'm being silly and I envision who it's really about. Will. The pain of what he's done hits me again and I sit up. No, I will not apologise for having feelings. Not anymore. Not then and not now. 'Yes, it was a long time ago. I know that, and I've very much moved on from it. But I never said it at the time and now I'm saying it. I'm not keeping it in any longer. It hurt my feelings, it wasn't okay, and it wasn't kind. Yes, we were kids but you shouldn't have done it.'

Teddy pulls himself up onto his haunches. 'You're blowing this way out of proportion; we were *little* kids.' He's breezy now, back to his laidback demeanour.

I change tack. 'Do you have a girlfriend, Teddy?' I ask.

His smile lights up his face, happy to be on safer ground. 'Yes, and a baby girl.' There's a gentleness in his voice now.

'How would you feel if someone did that to your little girl. She loved him and he hurt her. How would you feel?'

His face drops and there's a small vein throbbing on his temple, it's the only sign that he feels anything. It shows the fury that's there, it's subtle but I see it. Finally, after a while of contemplation he responds.

'I'm sorry I hurt your feelings.' He keeps the warmth in his voice as he says it, not just going through the motions to appease me, he's thinking of his baby girl getting her feelings hurt. Now he understands and that's all I needed.

That's all I needed to remind myself that he is not Will, who I'm really mad at. That he did hurt my feelings back then, but it was a long time ago and I've more than moved on. Regardless, I feel a great sense of closure and I think back to when we were little and he was the boy who liked my hair and I smile.

'Can I book another session?'

Chapter 12

Dotty laughs as I tell her about my brush with death, okay so maybe I embellished it a little but I felt pretty scared at the time. It's those proper belly laughs, right from the gut and I get caught up in it too, my sides screaming for me to stop but every time I look at Dotty a fresh set of giggles escape. It's most cathartic.

I find myself laughing here a lot more than I used to with Eloise or with Will. Theirs were 'in' jokes and fun but we never really laughed like this, when I think back, I can't help but wince over how I was probably one of those 'in' jokes. I wonder if they're doing belly-laughs over me now. My smile freezes on my face as I let my thoughts drift back to them as they so often have over the last week.

'Okay love?' Dotty asks, placing a huge cup of tea on the kitchen table in front of me, a Dotty special as I think of it now.

She makes the same cup of tea regardless of who's here and regardless of what they ask her for.

She was making a cup for the postman when she said, 'I know how to make one really good cup of tea and that's what I make, none of this fannying about with different milks, sweeteners and amounts of sugar. That tea is tried and tested, it's just right and it's how I make it. No one ever says anything, but they always drink it.' She twinkled at me then.

I just can't get over how much I enjoy Dotty's company; she knows her own mind, and she's unapologetic. I always make sure everyone has exactly what they ask for and almost feel anxiety if I don't make it right and here's Dotty making whatever she likes and everyone can like it or lump it.

'Yes, I'm fine.' I bring myself back to the present, trying to readjust my face. I've not mentioned Will or Eloise since that first fateful night and I'm grateful that Dotty hasn't brought them up either. Even though she knows what happened, there's something about her not being there to witness my humiliation or knowing Will and Eloise, that makes it easier to cope with. Back home it would be the elephant in every room, here it's just the little mouse, sometimes it's scratching at the walls, sometimes it's happily chewing away on some cheese but it's always there, just quieter. Subdued.

'Are you off out with my Joe this evening then?' Dotty changes the subject, raising her eyebrows so they disappear under her soft grey curls.

'Yes,' I say, feeling shy and slightly self-conscious; he's her grandson but it's just friendly. Nothing serious, even if he does end every message with a kiss. That's normal though, right? Just friendly. I'm not his type.

As if they've been summoned, I hear a calling from the hallway. It sounds like Joe but as he enters the room, two little girls skipping in his wake, well one skipping and the other half-skipping, half-hopping, I see that it's Max. I try to hide the disappointment from my face, I look beyond Max, ready to see Joe bringing up the rear but he's not there. The door closes and I attempt to stop my mouth from dropping. I'm more disappointed than I thought I would be.

'The door was unlocked so we let ourselves in,' he says, pointedly. I don't know how I could have mistaken him for Joe, his voice is similar, but his tone is much cooler, harsher even.

'Hello dear, tea?' Dotty signals to the freshly brewed pot and Max nods along in his ever-grumpy way.

'Granny, Granny!' The girls dance around in the kitchen, excited as ever. 'I'm hungry,' Hazel announces with Neve echoing 'Hungee' and hopping about after her sister.

'My gosh you two are always hungry, is your Daddy not feeding you?' Dotty play acts casting a pretend disapproving look over at Max.

'They had some toast, not even thirty minutes ago.' He shrugs, chuckling at his little girls, his face momentarily softening.

'Where's Joe? Did he not travel down with you?' Dotty asks. I'm so pleased; I'd been wondering the same myself but dare not ask.

'Think he had some bits to do for work, he'll be down later.' He rolls his eyes. 'How have you been doing this week, Gran?' He looks over at me suspiciously. I stop myself from rolling *my* eyes, what has made this man so unpleasant?

'Granny where's the nakey woman?' Hazel asks and we all laugh, no guile.

'She's sat just there.' Dotty raises her long finger and points at me.

Hazel appraises me. 'You look different and your clothes are different.' She's almost accusing me of something. Neve watches me with her big blue eyes, 'different' she repeats, echoing Hazel's tone and squinting at me.

'Thank you,' I say, grinning at her, happy to have someone notice.

'I liked the funny towel,' she says finally and there's a round of cackles again. It even makes Max laugh.

Max stays for a quick tense breakfast and then makes some noises about needing to attend to something or other and his general irritation that Joe isn't here.

'Just leave the girls with us, you don't mind helping me do you, Anna?'

'Of course,' I say, wondering what could possibly be so important that he needs to go off again and leave the girls. Where's their mum?

Perhaps she's up in London still doing some posh, important job, probably some kind of model. All tall and long with harsh angles and pointy elbows, I can imagine her now. Probably has the same matching scowling face hidden behind a mop of perfect hair. Or maybe she's softer, warmer, fun, someone like the girls which would explain why they're so lovely. Whoever she is she's a saint to put up with Max.

'Are you sure? I'm sorry to do this, I'm so annoyed with Joe I thought he would be here too, to help,' he grumbles.

'I can help,' I say defiantly, feeling like a petulant child who can't be trusted to help out with the family chores.

'Um yes, okay. Thank you.' He clears his throat awkwardly. 'I'll be back in a few hours girls.' He leans down to their level and looks them both in the eyes.

'Oh Daddy,' Hazel whines and Neve echoes.

'I know, it's just a few hours and then we'll have some fun together. I promise.'

The girls both throw their little arms around his neck practically hanging off him and he envelops them in a huge hug. He may be an arse, but at least he's a good dad.

'I love you girls.' He looks at them both and kisses them gently on the cheeks. I think of my own dad, he would never be so open with his feelings. I knew he loved me but it wasn't something that was said in my house. It was known, but never said.

We decide to take the girls down to the beach, Hazel wants to look for shells and rocks and Neve wants to do anything that Hazel is doing and especially seems to like picking things up off the floor.

'I'll pack some snacks, shall I?' I ask Dotty, thinking about how unpleasant children can be when hungry. Then thinking how unpleasant some adults can be when they're hungry.

Perhaps that's why Eloise was a bit of a bitch, she could be kind and fun but she also had a pernickety, self-obsessed side that she hid pretty well but the more I think back the more I see it. It was always about Eloise and what she wanted. I don't know why I'm surprised she took Will from me; she wanted him so she had him just like everything else. When we were younger and we used to go clubbing, men would look over at us and she was always convinced they were looking at her.

'Why is that man looking at me?' she would ask and I wouldn't even think about it. Of course, he was looking at her, but it would have been nice if she thought he could have been looking at me, perhaps he was interested in me.

She hated people being late but she'd always be at least ten minutes late for everything herself. If she happened to get there first, she'd moan and complain about people wasting her time. She was always beautifully dressed but it would take her so long to get ready, you could never just quickly get ready and go; her outfit would have to be perfect. She'd have everything ironed and couldn't understand why anyone wouldn't but not everyone could afford a cleaner and pay them extra for ironing.

Dotty takes Neve to change her nappy as Hazel hovers over me while I make some snacks and pop them inside Dotty's bag.

'That looks nice,' she says and literally licks her lips. 'Nene can't have these.' She indicates most of the snacks.

'I think that's up to your granny, isn't it?' I appease, not wishing to get into any disagreements with a child about who can have what.

'Okay.' She smiles.

Chapter 13

Down on the beach we find an array of shells, stones and rocks. The girls are so pleased and want to take them all back but Dotty refuses.

'It's been fun finding them but if everyone took the shells off the beaches there would be none left, you can each take one and a few rocks,' she lectures gently.

'Hmmm, okay. Can we at least hide the rest?' Hazel pleads, crossing her arms in front of her, clearly unhappy with Granny's decision.

'Well of course, would be no fun for anyone to find them otherwise.'

The girl's squabble over the few that they will take back to Dotty's and we spend the next half an hour hiding the remaining shells all over the beach.

'This one should go over there.' Hazel points to a little rock pool down on the other side of the beach.

'I think it would be fine here.' I try to pacify her but Hazel is insistent; she's certainly headstrong, she clenches her fists and I feel a tantrum coming on.

'It needs to go out there,' she insists, thrusting her index finger at the rocks again.

There are quite a lot of rocks to get over to the rock pool she has chosen, painstakingly pointing it out and ensuring I know exactly which one she means. I finally agree and Hazel seems placated; tantrum avoided.

'On one condition,' I tell her. 'That you stay on the beach with Granny and Neve.'

She nods triumphantly. The last thing I need is Hazel or Neve to be scrambling over the slippery rocks and hurting themselves. No thank you. Imagine Max's fury if I was responsible for one of his children getting hurt.

I start to scramble over the rocks wondering what I'm doing with myself. How did this little girl get me to do this? I need to find more guts. I need to say no to people, like I did with Teddy. Where's the Anna who speaks her mind now?

The sludgy stuff on the rocks allows no grip, I'm nearly there when my foot suddenly slips. It gives me a little jolt, but I manage to regain my balance, focusing on where I need to go and what I need to do. I'm almost there now, might as well do it. I stay still for a minute refocusing, listening to the sounds of the ocean and the seagulls squawking above.

I take a deep breath and another foot forward. I can do this, it's not like it's Everest for goodness' sake. Finally, I'm here and I place the little shell in the rock pool. Chuffed with myself I turn back and call to the girls that I've done it! I hear the girls cheering, their little arms in the air and a little dance from Neve, they look so sweet.

'Woohoo,' I scream, my mouth hanging open, completely caught up in the moment until I feel a splat across my face and into my open mouth.

I try to work out what it is. Looking down at the waves and moving my hand up towards my face I spit with force when I realise. Spit, spit, spit. I put my hand in the water and pull it up to my mouth to wash it out, the taste of salt now hitting my tongue as well as the taste of something much worse. I look up and there they are circling above as if mocking me. I wash the rest of my face and hair in the water desperately trying to get the seagull poo off me, feeling disgusting. Why on my face? Why in my mouth?

Having done the best I can, I scramble quickly back to the girls and Dotty, occasionally glancing up at the offending gulls, afraid they will start to pelt me with more. Bastards.

'Daddy you should have seen it, it was so funny. The seagull went splat on her face.' Hazel mimics the action, using both hands to show the huge splat.

'Splat, splat.' Neve dances, bringing her hands up to her face as though she's playing peekaboo.

I come back down the stairs, trying to ignore the story being told in the hallway and head into the kitchen. I'm craving a cup of Dotty tea now.

'Here you are, love.' There's a curl to Dotty's lips that shows her amusement but she's trying her best not to laugh. 'I bet that was the best shower ever.'

'Oh yes and I've brushed my teeth ten times.' I

roll my eyes.

'Freshest breath ever.' She giggles, and I start to giggle too. Thinking about how it must have looked to them, how ridiculous the whole thing was.

Max comes and sits down at the table, a clear smirk on his face, it's the most amused I've seen his moody face since I met him.

'I heard you had, ahem, fun down at the beach.' And there it is, the little sparkle that seems to be in all of their eyes. Is it a Cornish thing?

'You could say that.' I groan, not giving him an inch.

In true Dotty style she pops a cup of tea down for Max.

'Would you mind getting my bag for me Max, my pills are in it.'

'It's in the hallway,' I say. It was heavy, lugging it back up to the house.

'Sure,' he pops out and then a few seconds later I hear him calling. 'Are you sure it's here? I can't see it.'

Dotty and I exchange a universal look, knowing that as soon as one of us goes out there we will spot it right away.

Dotty goes to head out but I stand up before she does. 'I'll go, I remember putting it down, it's probably right under his nose.'

I go through to hallway and Max's stern looking face is back on. 'I can't see it anywhere,' he says, there's something accusatory about his tone.

'It's just here,' I say, trying to reach down to where I'd left it only it's not there anymore. I rack my brain; I know I was distracted by the bird poo but I know I carried it back here and I remember putting it in the hallway before I hurried upstairs to get clean.

I come back through to the kitchen.

'Did you move the bag, Dotty, and perhaps forget?' I ask, softly.

'No dear, I've not touched my bag, it's not out in the hallway then?'

'No, it's not.' Max comes up behind me. 'Let's have a look around the house, maybe you put it somewhere else.' He looks meaningfully at me and I really want to punch his smug, stupid face, after I find the bag of course.

We spend the next hour turning the house upside down looking all over the place. Searching the hallway again and again and looking in the living room, even the bathroom; did I take it up to the shower? Could I have put it in the airing cupboard when I got a towel? It all gets a bit silly before we begin to come to the realisation that wherever the bag is, it's not here. Crap. And the second realisation that I am responsible. Double crap. I've replayed coming back from the beach in my head several times and I just can't make sense of it.

Max helps Dotty freeze her debit and credit cards in case it's been taken by someone and the whole time he keeps eyeing me, blaming me every step of the way. This man does not like me one little bit. His passive aggressive comments and hints are becoming less passive the more time goes on.

To make matters worse the girls are bouncing

around with all the anxious excitement that is going on and Max is growing more impatient and angrier by the minute, it's as though he thinks I took the bag and hid it.

'Woof, woof,' Hazel comes over on all fours playing dog with a little Neve dog in her wake, woofing loudly.

'Not now, Hazel,' Max snaps. 'We need to find Granny's bag that someone lost.' He says someone but we all know he means me. I'm surprised he's being so polite.

'Woof, woof,' she starts again.

Max sighs and continues to look, ignoring Hazel's attempt to play. Undeterred she heads over in my direction.

'Woof, woof,' she says to me with Neve echoing her barks.

'Not now, I'll play once we find the bag,' I appease, turning my attention away.

'Woof, woof, I'm a sniffer dog, I can sniff it out,' she says.

Max's head pops up and we exchange a curious look.

'You can sniff it out?' he asks Hazel and she woofs in response.

'Go dog, go,' I scream as we both realise and watch transfixed as Hazel and Neve run over to the curtain and pull it back to reveal Granny's bag.

'Hazel, did you hide Granny's bag?' Max's anger has slightly dissipated and he keeps his tone soft and even. As he moves the bag out there are a few wrappers behind it, I think back to this morning and

Hazel coveting the snacks I was packing. I'm so relieved I don't even care that she hid it, I could laugh over it all.

'No,' she says pushing her lip out. 'It was Nene.'

'It wasn't, was it? It's okay, just tell the truth. You know we don't like lies.'

'Okay, Daddy, it was me. Nene isn't allowed those snacks though.' She huffs, crossing her arms across her chest. 'I told her that.'

'You do know we've been looking for that bag for the last hour,' Max scolds.

She pops her head down. 'Sorry, Daddy, sorry Anna.' She says it so sweetly it's almost impossible to stay mad. Is it any wonder she has everyone wrapped around her little finger.

'We'll talk about this later young lady, but that was very naughty. You had all of us worried about where it was, and it had Granny's pills and her purse in it. That was not okay.'

'Sorry,' she mumbles, her lip beginning to wobble.

'You better go and apologise to Granny and that's no Granny cake for you this afternoon. You don't need it after all those snacks.'

'Harumph,' she grumbles, but goes back through to Granny without another word.

Neve follows Hazel back through the house to go to see Granny too.

'Ahem,' Max croaks. 'Sorry about that.'

'Sorry that you thought I stole Dotty's bag? Or sorry about how rude you've been to me? And not just today.' I raise my eyebrows, waiting for an answer, like a headmistress telling off a gobby teen.

Max looks startled but before he has a chance to answer I head back through to the kitchen to the sound of laughter. Clearly Hazel has been forgiven.

Chapter 14

I offer to go out and do a spot of shopping for Dotty, a quick message from Joe lets me know he won't be in town before six. I have a few hours to kill and no desire to be in Max's company.

Joe's been messaging me over the week, suggesting places I should visit around town and checking in on Dotty. I can't help but feel excited by him. It's like having a hot texting tour guide. He's such fun and so light compared to Max's doom and gloom, I don't know how they can be so different. Then there's Dotty, I can see so much of her in Joe but not surly Max. There's no fun in Max, aside from the odd occasion with his girls, perhaps he saves it all for them.

'Sorry about Max, he's very protective of me, too much sometimes and he got the wrong end of the stick. He's embarrassed, I assure you and I never thought for one moment you had hidden the bag anywhere,' Dotty tells me, but I don't want to hear it or speak of him.

The shopping is a welcome distraction. I'll have some time to myself and then I only have to suffer him for a few hours before I'll be out, and he'll go back to wherever he came from. It'll be good to be back to just me and Dotty. I've tried not to think too far beyond this next week but as more days go by the idea of going back to work and dealing with Eloise horrifies me. I know I can't hide away here forever, and this little land of limbo is only prolonging the inevitable. I will have to go and face the music soon; I just wish I knew what the song was.

I meander down the aisles slowly, taking my time over the list Dotty gave me. There's no rush. I'm finishing up choosing individual potatoes very carefully, only the best will do for his highness, when I turn and bump into someone. I'm looking down at some huge feet, big, black trainers with a white, green and blue stripe steps one way and then the other in a kind of clumsy dance. Feeling irritated I look up flustered.

'Excuse me,' I say, irritated. I'm not ready to take anyone's crap after my encounter with Max.

'Anna?' The man greets me, and I move my attention to his eyes, it takes me a while of just staring before I can put a name to the face. Jared. My first real boyfriend.

While Teddy has grown into a surfer hunk with a brooding charm and a chilled-out spirit, Jared has not fared so well. In the approximately fifteen years since I've seen him, he has developed a bit of a paunch around the middle and his hair is thinning badly on top. He could do with accepting it and shaving the hair but instead he has tried to comb it over, to no avail, there's no covering the mass of baldness and the hairs that remain are gelled down in a vain attempt to hide his scalp. He's dressed in a track suit that appears to match his odd trainers.

'Anna? It is you? What are you doing here? This is so weird.' His face spreads into a huge grin, the cat that got the cream.

'Jared?' I ask, still disbelieving that it's him. Perhaps a relative of his.

'Yes, it's me. Do you live down here?' He shakes his head not believing his eyes either and leans in closer than I'd like. I catch a whiff of *Lynx* and am momentarily transported back to the ice rink, skating circles around one another until he chose to skate them around someone else.

'No just visiting, do you?' I ask, and he nods. What are the chances. Jared. Have all my old boyfriends come here?

'You don't fancy going out for a drink or a coffee or something?' he ventures, raising his eyebrows in what would have been a seductive way in his heyday.

A girl has got some time to waste and I'll admit I want to find out how he ended up like this. Curiosity and a wish to be as far away from Max as possible makes me agree.

'Just a quick coffee would be great, it's nice to catch up with old friends,' I clarify subtly, this is definitely *not* a date.

We both pay for our shopping, his seems to mainly consist of beer and crisps and instead of heading out the doors to the local *Costa* Jared guides me to the supermarket's café which is in serious need of an update. The walls are a sad shade of magnolia washed with grease and crayon presumably from little kids drawing on them. The menu is wanting and the chairs are sticky plastic, but it's not a date and just a drink, so it'll do.

'How do you like your coffee?' he asks, but I settle on a tea instead and find myself rattling off how Dotty makes it. I'm a true convert. Jared buys himself a coffee and a chocolate muffin which he takes a huge bite out of the second we sit down.

'Anna, Anna, Anna.' Jared draws out my name, cake crumbs sticking to his teeth and falling from his mouth. From the young Jared I'd have found this charming; this older version doesn't have the same affect. He shuffles in his seat opposite me and I recognise the look he has on his face. 'It's been what, ten years?'

'More like fifteen,' I correct, thinking how even though he looks very different to the handsome fifteen-year-old he was, he still has the same sleazy attitude, and confidence in abundance. How is it that some people just have that?

'Yes of course,' he concedes. 'Tell me about your life. Married? Kids? I can't believe it Anna, one of my school girlfriends. It's so good to see you.'

I shake my head no to his barrage of questions and smile.

'Woah, I'd have thought you'd be all sprogged up by now, better get to it. Not getting any younger are we.'

And like that I wish I'd gone straight back to Dotty's, a visit with Max is much better than a conversation about my womb and how many child bearing years I have left. Why do people think it's an acceptable route of conversation?

Despite my silence Jared is not deterred and goes into detail about his own life. He's been married once, divorced, has two children by two women, one is the ex-wife and one he cheated on the ex-wife with. He holds no shame over it, conversationally dropping it in like it's an acceptable way to treat people, like cheating is okay, the norm, what everyone does. Is it the norm? I think about the last time we were together, skating around the rink before I caught him kissing someone else at the lockers. I had loved skating but I stopped; Mum couldn't understand it. I cringe thinking about how I snapped at her to stay out of it and I just didn't like it anymore, people change their minds. After that I'd see him around the town sometimes, but I'd be sure not to look and he never came to see me. He never apologised and I never said anything to him. I let him treat me like a doormat. He's mid-sentence through all his health issues when I come to a realisation.

'You're an arsehole,' I blurt, and I enjoy the millisecond it takes for Jared to stop talking and the shock to register on his face. His mouth drops open, half-masticated muffin swirling around in there. He's vile.

'There's no need to be a bitch, I'm not an arsehole. I just bought you a tea,' he moans, gruffly.

'Yes, you are, that's exactly what you are. You were an arsehole back when we were together, and you're an arsehole now. You cheated on me and that's what you continue to do. You've not learned anything.' I take a big gulp of my tea, my mouth suddenly dry. I don't know why I'm staying but I want to hear what he has to say for himself.

'I don't need this shit,' he spits. 'You're as bad as my ex-wife, you are.' He's loud and loutish, the few people in the café look over at us.

'If she has a brain I probably am. Sounds like the best thing she ever did was leave you.' I keep my voice light and sweet, not wishing to get into a shouting match with this brute.

'Oh my God, I found someone else, so sue me. Get over it. It was a long time ago. I was young. Everyone got with everyone back then.'

'I know it was a long time ago and I'm well over it, thank you very much but I'm doing this new thing where I say what I want to say.' I think of Dotty and take a deep breath. 'I should have said something back then but fifteen-year-old me was too chicken and didn't like confrontation.' I take another deep breath. 'It was an arsehole thing going off with another girl; you should have finished it with me before you started something with someone else. Perhaps you could try and take that away as a life lesson?'

'I don't need your life lessons; you were so insecure. How do I know you wasn't cheating on me?' He raises his voice slightly, regaining the attention of those sitting around.

'I never cheated on you, why is it cheats need to try and tarnish everyone else with the same brush? Well guess what, there are people who don't cheat. Decent people,' I say with conviction. '*I* am not an arsehole and don't blame me for your cheating. You cheated because you're selfish and because you wanted to have your cake and eat it.'

'If you hadn't...' he starts, and I put my hand up to cut him off.

'No, you will not gaslight me. I don't care about what you have to say. You were in the wrong, you should have told me it was over before starting something with someone else, and you are a selfish arsehole. Goodbye Jared.' And before another word has a chance to spout from his gobshite mouth I waltz out of there. Ready to go back to see Dotty.

I was wanting for an argument and Jared turned up at just the right time. Max has had a lucky escape.

I take a deep breath, inhaling happiness, exhaling anger.

Chapter 15

I head back to the house with a slight skip in my step. No one can beat me now. I've told off Teddy and Jared, who knows what's next but a moody arsehole like Max certainly won't bother me. I can handle him.

As I open the door, I hear Max and Dotty, further up the hallway, deep in conversation in a very hushed tone. They're not aware of my presence and I can't help but listen.

'It's been awful, Hazel has been crying over mummy almost every night. I just don't know what to do for the best,' he mumbles.

'You're doing your best love,' says Dotty comfortingly. 'It's been almost two years and she remembers before, it's difficult for her, this whole thing is probably easier for Neve, at least she doesn't remember her properly.'

'You're right, it's been really difficult for us all. I feel like we're beginning to work through it now but it's a real struggle at times.'

'Understandably,' Dotty whispers.

I close the door with purpose and hear their conversation stop abruptly. I feel guilty for eavesdropping. Almost two years? Hazel and Neve's Mum is dead? It makes sense as to why they've hardly spoken about her. I feel so awful for them, I can't help but look at poor Max in a new light. My heart goes out to those little girls growing up without a mother. My eyes begin to well at the sadness of it all. A renewed respect for Max begins to form, perhaps that's why he's such a stick in the mud. Perhaps if my partner had died, I'd be like that too. I view him now with new eyes, endeavouring to let the handbag incident go. He was just trying to look out for Dotty after all. Perhaps Max was more like his light-hearted brother before all this happened. I feel awful for judging him so unkindly, not that he's made it easy to like him.

I head into the kitchen to find Neve sitting on Joe's lap giggling and bouncing around on his knee whilst Hazel expertly applies a layer of lipstick to his face, it's clearly not his first layer and he looks hilarious and a bit sticky.

'Hello, sorry I'm later than we planned. Still on for tonight though?' Joe gives me a big grin and it's impossible not to return the smile, he looks ridiculous.

'Nearly finished Uncle Joe, shall I do your face next, Anna?' Hazel's eyes light up and she turns to me, I cast my eyes over Joe's multicoloured face, the makeup has been used more like face paint, it'll take some scrubbing to get it all off.

'Umm, perhaps another time, Hazel, I need to grab a shower.'

'You don't look stinky.' Hazel comes over sniffing the air around me. She stands unnecessarily close and inhales deeply. 'You're fine.'

'Don't sniff the guests, Hazel,' Max says, placing a big cup of tea in front of me.

'She said she needed a wash, Daddy. I was just checking.' Hazel's little face contorts into a pout.

'Just checking, Daddy,' Neve repeats sweetly, scrunching up her little nose and attempting to sniff me too. She gets a little too close though, her face in my skirt and I give her a little pat, this sweet girl without a mum.

'Perhaps Daddy would like some makeup girls.' Joe smirks at me.

'No. No Daddy would not.' Back to his usual stick in the mud self.

I can't help it. 'Daddy does seem like he could do with some makeup.'

His eyes flash. 'Oh God, don't you start.' His tone is almost cutting.

The evening with Joe is the best distraction. He's kind, attentive and funny, the perfect mix of hot and charming. Nothing like Will and everyone knows there's nothing like a new man to forget an old one. I find myself laughing so much it feels good to be out socialising again.

'So come on, I feel like I hardly know anything about you.' He waits wide-eyed for my response.

'Not much to say really.' I find myself fluttering

my eyelashes at him.

'I'm sure that's not true, I think there's a lot more to you than meets the eye. That's how it is with Max you know. He's a nice man, he's not had the easiest of times so please don't take it too personally when he's a bit,' he looks up searching for the right word, 'protective.'

'I understand, don't worry. It can't be easy with everything he's been through.' I lower my eyes, feeling guilty at my earlier unintended snooping.

He searches my face, clearly surprised. 'You know about Hazel and Neve's mum? Did Dotty tell you?'

It's too late. 'Umm, well, no. I overheard Max and Dotty talking. I wasn't eavesdropping I swear,' I confess.

'It's fine,' he smiles. 'It's a lot easier than having to talk about the whole sorry tale.'

I think about telling Joe about Will but I can't bear the thought of talking about him. Not here on my perfect date, so instead I keep the conversation light. We can cover this later, there's no rush, it's early days.

Joe tells me about his exciting life in London, the parties and people, his flat mates. He paints such a picture, making me feel included like I'm there with him. He's so easy to talk to and be around and his stories are such fun, it feels effortless to enjoy his company. He leans in as he describes the latest work deal he's passionate about; I breathe him in, earthy with a hint of mint. He smells divine. I think of my last close encounter with Jared; Joe smells like a real man not a boy covering his body odour.

'Are you staying at Dotty's tonight?' I ask. Already knowing the answer.

He nods along and I smile. The thoughts of seeing him over the breakfast table and getting to enjoy a bit more time with him making me feel excited.

'Do you want to do something tomorrow?' I ask, feeling bold.

'Sure, sounds good. I should hopefully have time before I head back.'

We start the walk back to Dotty's. It's getting dark and the stars are beginning to come out. I love how little light pollution there is here, you can see so much more of the night sky. It strikes me that this is one of the most romantic dates I've ever been on. Will wasn't one for romance really, or maybe he was with Eloise. Enthused and strong from my recent confrontations I decide to do something unlike me, to take the lead and kiss Joe. I watch him as he talks about some of the places he's travelled to and the experiences he's had. As he turns his face towards mine, I put my hand on his cheek and pull him down into a kiss. I barely have a second to enjoy it before it's over and he's moving my hand from his face, a startled expression in his eyes.

'Oh Anna, I'm so sorry,' he's saying. 'I thought you knew?'

'Knew what?'

'I'm gay,' he responds simply.

I rush away, head for the beach, Joe calling my name from behind me telling me it's okay but I don't look back. I don't want to be around Joe.

'I need some time on my own,' I yell back. 'It's fine.'

And it is fine, but it doesn't stop me from being utterly mortified. It must've been a combination of the drink and a good-looking man. What was I thinking? I'm nowhere near ready to move on from Will. I drop down on the sand and shake my head.

I've barely sat down for ten minutes when I feel a presence next to me.

'What brings you down here?' His arm swings limply by his side, a bag for life in his hand, my least favourite man and just the person I did not want to see, Max is looming over me.

'Oh, I just wanted to watch the waves,' I say, lamely. Focusing my attention on the water lapping at the shore.

'I see,' he says, offering me a lopsided grin and plopping himself down next to me on the sand. 'I feel I owe you a big apology,' he starts.

'You already apologised, it's fine,' I say, hoping that'll put a stop to it.

'No, no it's not fine. I am sorry about the way I've been with you. It's just been a difficult time with everything and their mum...' He clears his throat and tries again 'Their mum...' I can see he's at pains to tell me, so I put him out of his misery.

'You don't have to tell me, I know. I heard you and Dotty talking about her and then Joe mentioned it a little.' I look at him apologetically, but I can see he's not angry. 'I wasn't trying to listen, I'm sorry for eavesdropping.' I feel my face redden.

'No, it's okay, it makes it kind of easier not to have to go over it all again.' He pulls his hand through his thick hair.

I smile at him, showing I understand, but how can you understand losing a spouse. The poor man.

'Do you want some crips?' he asks shuffling around in his bag and pulling out a few bags.

'Crips?'

'Sorry, it's what the girls call them, especially Neve.'

'Ah, I see you had a wild night planned then.'

'Yes.' He smirks. 'I was planning on watching the waves. Girls are in bed and it's nice to be able to have some time to myself. Clear my head.'

'Do you want me to leave you to it?' I ask, wondering if he's trying to hint that he'd rather be left alone. Although it was him who joined me.

'No, no. It's lovely here, I'm sure we can sit and enjoy it together.' His voice is softer, not as stiff as I'm used to. It's nice.

Chapter 16

'You really didn't realise Joe is gay?' Max rolls around in the sand clutching his side, his shoulders moving up and down as he laughs.

'Well, no.' I fold my arms, irritated at Max's obvious joy. I obviously have no gaydar, or cheating-dar if that's a thing. I'm hopeless. I sigh loudly not even trying to hide it. Who cares, I can't do anything right by Max anyway so I'll just say it how it is, that's what I do now. The new me.

'So, what did he do when you tried to kiss him?' Max's eyes twinkle with mischief and he stops laughing.

I cover my face. I'm regretting telling Max about our non-kiss now, he already thinks I'm an idiot. 'He kind of pushed me away,' I mumble through my hands.

He pulls his lips in stifling a giggle but a loud snort escapes.

'I know, I'm pathetic!' I shriek.

I lie back on the sand and look up at the sky, it's

late and the stars are fully out, they're astoundingly clear.

'I'm sorry. He's been out since he was fourteen, he's very comfortable in his own skin.'

I side eye Max, still unsure if I want to continue this conversation. He's right about Joe, he really does know himself, Max doesn't seem like his brother in that way. Perhaps Max and I are a bit more alike than I thought.

'He was very... attentive and I got the wrong idea. I don't understand why Dotty didn't tell me though.' I harumph.

'Oh, she doesn't know. Didn't Joe say?'

'Really? Dotty doesn't seem like she would care.' I think of the warmth and kindness she has offered to me and I can't imagine anything but acceptance coming from her. Although my first impression of her might have been quite different in her drab clothes. Now I know her she's the most wonderful person.

'She's from a different generation. I think it's more in Joe's head really.' He shrugs. 'He's worried she wouldn't accept him; they've always been thick as thieves. You know Joe is our grandad's namesake and I think Gran always envisioned him settling down and having kids, much in the same way they did.'

'I'm sure Dotty cares most about his happiness though, and he could still have kids.'

'Yes, I know and I'm sure you're right. I've said the same to Joe but it's his place to tell her, not mine. I always thought he was waiting for someone special enough to make it worth it, none of his relationships have lasted long enough to introduce anyone to the family.'

I smile at him respecting his brother's wishes. They might tease each other but they really seem close.

'You're a good brother and dad.' It slips shyly out before I have a chance to think about it. He is an amazing dad though, it's true.

'Thanks, and you're a good carer. It's not been easy.'

I nod in a knowing way; it mustn't have been. I don't speak, allowing him to speak if he wants to. We watch the waves in a very comfortable way and I marvel at the romance again, cringing at the memory of my attempted kiss with Joe. I won't be doing that again in a hurry.

When Max and I get back to the house, Joe is sitting in the kitchen with, invariably, a Dotty brew placed in front of him and another next to it.

'Ah, the wanderers return. I was hoping to have a word, Anna.' Joe's tone is soft and he motions to me with his head whilst looking at Max. My cheeks colour thinking of our last encounter. Why oh why does everyone have to be staying here? Why have I made everything into such a mess? I've run away from one mess and created another. I glance between the brothers as a moment passes between them.

Max nods along patting his brother on the back and giving me a small smile.

'I'll leave you two to it but, Anna, would you like to spend the day with me, the girls and Dotty tomorrow?'

I'm startled by his invitation; it seems so unlike him and I spy Joe looking curiously between us.

'I'd love to.' And this time I really mean it.

'I'm off to bed. I'll leave you two to chat,' he says, a small smirk playing on his lips. Damn him.

Alone with Joe, I find myself looking over at him, he is handsome there's no denying that. I definitely think the rebounds were calling and I'm psyching myself up to say something along those lines when Joe cuts in.

'Don't sweat it, it's happened before. You don't get to be this good looking without a few girls throwing themselves at you.'

In spite of myself I giggle and the atmosphere is broken.

'What's a kiss between friends anyway?' He searches my eyes as he says this, it's more of a question, checking we're friends and it pleases me that he's not running a million miles away.

'I'm sorry I got the wrong end of the stick,' I say, feeling the heat in my cheeks as I remember my monumental error.

'It's my fault too,' he says kindly. 'I could see you weren't from around here; you seemed a bit lost and perhaps needed a friend. If I'm honest this isn't the first time a girl has misread my friendly nature and I'm down here so often at the moment, it was nice to hang out with someone I'm not related to.' He shrugs. 'So, friends?'

'Yes, friends,' I confirm, feeling slightly less awkward.

'Just don't mention it to Gran please,' he pleads.

'I know it's none of my business, but you should tell Dotty. She'd be fine with it, it's the twenty-first century!'

'I know, and you're right. It's just never been the right time and there's not really been anyone special enough to make it worth it.'

'I think perhaps on some level she knows.' I think back to Dotty telling me I wasn't his type. She really wasn't kidding.

Dotty isn't feeling well the following day and opts to stay in bed, Joe decides to stay with her and I'm relieved. Even though we've made up I still feel little flushes of shame as I picture Joe's rejection. Joe and Dotty insist I go with Max and the kids for a day at the zoo. I say the zoo but the place we go to is so enormous it even has a safari trail, a train and a boat. It's not somewhere I would normally visit; Will would much rather play golf over the weekend or we'd go out for dinner, but I love the idea of spending the day with Neve and Hazel, they're little bundles of joy.

We spend the day exploring the animals with the kids. Neve is a big monkey fan and she's most looking forward to going to see them on the safari, which we decide to save until last so we can make the drive back to Dotty's after.

'You're really good with the girls.' Max smiles at me and I grin back, sincerely now.

It's funny how my opinion of him has changed so much after our heart-to-heart last night and I can physically feel that he has relaxed in my company. He's not quite so stern now and the children absolutely adore him. He picks Neve up and pops her on his shoulders, her little arms are wrapped around his head as he wanders around pointing out the animals.

'Thanks, they're lovely and so sweet.' I ruffle Hazel's hair and she puts her little hand in mine.

She perks up, sensing an opportunity and batting her little eyelashes. 'Daddy, please can we go to the park?'

'Park, Daddy?' Neve repeats, banging on Max's head like a drum.

'Yes, in a little bit.' He groans in an indulgent way. These little girls must always get their own way.

We're finally ready to go around the safari trail. The girls both come up to the front of the car and sit on my lap so they can see everything as we barely move a few miles an hour, stopping occasionally so we can watch the animals. We enjoy the giraffes, elephants and emus then it's time to go into the monkey enclosure. Neve and Hazel's excitement is palpable and they're both bouncing around on my knees. With the first monkey jumping onto the windscreen Neve screams and buries her tiny face in my shoulder.

'It's okay, it's just a monkey. It's exciting to see them, isn't it, Hazel?' I try to encourage Hazel.

'Can they get in the car? Oh, he's jumped on the

top of the car, Neve,' Hazel practically yells and Neve buries her head further into my shoulder, butting her head into my face in the process.

'Ouch,' I grumble.

'Oh, sorry about little concrete head there, it's a wonder you've not been headbutted before really.'

'Concrete head?'

'A loving nickname of course.' Max flashes a smile at me, his fun side shining through at last.

Looking at him makes my stomach betray me by flipping itself. What is that about? I remind myself about the last time I listened to my obviously still rebounding stomach flip. No, he's just a handsome friend. Pull yourself together, Anna.

Another two monkeys jump onto the car, one on the bonnet and the other on the roof. The one on the roof is making a real racket.

'What's it doing up there?'

'Probably trying to pull off my antenna.' Max sighs. 'Last time we came they almost pulled the wing mirror off.'

I look at him, horrified. 'Oh my God, and you came back?'

'Neve hasn't been before and she loves monkeys, how could I resist?'

I'm suddenly reminded of Will's car which is still in the garage; I really must retrieve and return it to him. He'll be going mad about it. He'd never bring his pride and joy through here, not even if he had kids who would love it.

'Let's all move around in the car and see if we can shake the monkey off?'

With that everyone begins to move, Neve cautiously peeking out but still very close to me, looking in wonderment at the monkeys. I don't know if I've seen her so quiet before.

Another jumps up and Hazel bursts out into giggles.

'Can we take one home, Daddy?'

'No, Hazel we can't, they live here. It wouldn't be safe.'

'Not safe,' Neve whispers into my shoulder and I rub her little back. She's so cuddly and sweet, poor little thing without a mother. I feel tears spring to my eyes at the thought of it. These sweet children, Max is doing an amazing job with them; they're happy and cheeky but it must be so difficult.

We get through the monkeys relatively unscathed until the last moment when one of the monkeys decides to do its business on the windscreen. The girls begin to scream and Max tries to bat it off with the windscreen wipers, smearing it all over as they go back and forth, back and forth. I cover my mouth but a huge snorting giggle ripples up and bursts from my mouth. The sound starts the girls off and before I know it, we're all in hysterics. Even Max has tears in his eyes from laughing. It takes us a while to get out of the monkey enclosure with battling between the laughter and the limited view from the windscreen.

One of the workers helpfully comes over and pours a bottle of water over the car and Max puts the windscreen cleaner on and it's off. Neve keeps repeating 'monkey poop on car' at an ever-increasing volume and every time we hear it we all laugh.

We grab a quick dinner on the way back to Dotty's and after saying goodbye to Granny, Max and Joe load the car up with a sleepy Neve and Hazel.

'Thank you for an amazing day,' I whisper, not wanting to rouse the children. I look at their little angelic faces and I can feel my eyes brim again.

'It was my pleasure. We've loved having you along with us. Thank you for coming and helping. It's been a great day. I'll be back in a week or so. We're planning on coming down for a holiday then before Hazel goes back to school at the end of the summer.'

It fills me with excitement to think about spending more time with them. Despite this, I stifle a yawn.

'Looks like they're not the only ones who are tired.'

'Yes, they've worn me out!'

'Let's stay in touch.' He leans in close, and I inhale his scent, it feels somewhat intimate, but then he gives me his card. So formal, so him, suddenly so far removed from the soft edges of the family man I saw earlier. Next, he'll be shaking my hand and thanking me for doing business with him.

'It has my mobile on it,' he says, by way of explanation and I nod in confirmation.

'Yes of course.' I feel a little deflated, but I don't know why. 'I'll see you soon Max, thanks again.' I walk slowly up to my room and lie down; I don't even get undressed; Max and the girls swirling around in my head.

Chapter 17

All that remains of Max and the girls are the crumbs around the chairs where the girls sit which makes me oddly sentimental. I imagine Hazel labouring over her food, talking between each bite, making her meal take an age, while Neve practically inhales her food before asking for more.

I glance at the large clock, taking in its loud ticks and Roman numerals; it's almost ten, my body must have fully adjusted to this lifestyle. I find the broom and give the floor a quick sweep. Busying myself making breakfast, toast and scrambled fresh eggs; my mouth waters and my stomach growls. I'm famished.

Normally I'd have been at work for hours already by now, having had a breakfast of dull porridge. Check-out is ten o'clock so around now there would be a rush of the last guests leaving. Cutting it fine. It's a great job for people watching, trying to work out their relationships to each other; couples, singles, man and wife, kids, we get them all.

Sometimes there's a lull between check-out and check-in and that's when I find it most difficult, especially if I need to be on the desk. I don't hate my job but it's a means to an end, the same as a lot of jobs are for most people, I suppose. I don't really know what I'd do with myself otherwise. My parents may have had their faults, but they were always hard workers, they instilled that in me too, and as much as I don't like to be like them, we share that. I work hard whilst people like Eloise go off and lead the exciting lives. Maybe not anymore.

Message to Anna
Thank you for spending the day with me and the girls yesterday. They've been raving about you ever since. Max

Message to Max
No problem, it was a lot of fun. Anna

Message to Anna
We should do something again when we're back down. Just trying to confirm my leave with work but should be a full week or two.

I don't like to admit it, even to myself, but by the time Max and the kids come back for that holiday I'll be back home trying to sort my sorry life out. I've avoided thinking about it but the thought of missing out on them has brought it all back up again. I don't know where to begin with everything that's happened. There's so much Max doesn't know. What would he think if he did? Would he pity me? I can't stand the thought of the pity in people's faces. So much to sort between Will and myself, to unpick our lives together, to separate what once was one.

Message to Max
Sounds great.

Message to Anna
Have you been kissing any strangers? Except my brother of course! X

Is he flirting with me? There's a kiss at the end of the message. What does this mean? Why am I overanalysing this? Should I put one back?

Message to Max
No I haven't cheeky! I try to save my kisses only for those that really deserve them. Aren't you working today? x

Message to Anna
No changing the subject. Work is very dull. xx

Message to Max
You better get back to it! xx

'Who's that who keeps messaging you? You're always on that thing now.' Dotty narrows her eyes at me, making me feel like a naughty schoolchild. Headmistress Dotty is back.

'Oh, no one.'

She lifts her chin up and down, pursing her lips but doesn't say anything. Does she know?

We're sitting in the living room, it's a cosy room, not the hub of the house like the kitchen but a comfortable room with two small, soft, patterned sofas. I'm sitting on one and Dotty on the other. I have my latest book laid out beside me, it's not a great read and I'm finding it hard to get into. Normally when I'm stressed a good book can make me forget but my mind is racing today, reality is pulling me back and I am loathe to go. Maybe I should go paddleboarding again, a bit of fresh air and the waves could do me good.

'Have you seen my reading glasses, dear?' Dotty looks around herself in a show of confusion and frustration.

I peer around me but don't see the round spectacles I'm used to seeing her wear.

'I've not seen them, want me to check the kitchen?' I offer, ready to go and search them out.

'No, I've already looked, there may be a pair right down the side of that sofa, in my knitting though. They're old but they'll do.'

'You knit?' I stare back at Dotty, wondering why I didn't know this.

'Not so much now, but I used to.'

I pull out a beautiful knitting bag from beside the sofa; I never noticed it before and open it to search out the alternative pair of glasses. There are loads of new balls of wool in there, the packaging still neatly round their middles. A few lines of a project, started but forgotten.

'This wool is lovely, what were you making?' I ask, as I rummage around for a glasses case.

'I can't remember now, do you knit?' she asks.

'No, but I do crochet,' I say quietly.

'Crochet? I tried that once, was awful at it, the hook might even be in there. Couldn't understand how you could do it without the other needle. Knitting's much easier.'

I locate Dotty's glasses and the crochet hook. She places them on her face with a smile.

'Much better, feel free to use all of that, I have more upstairs too, I won't be doing it. I was never that great at it anyway.'

'Are you sure?' I ask, appreciating the quality of the wool and how much it may have cost. My fingers are itching to start something now I have a hook.

'Yes, definitely, no point it going to waste.'

Dotty picks up her book, the conversation ends and I search through the knitting bag for inspiration of what to crochet.

The next week goes by in a blur of crochet, messages, paddle boarding and Dotty. It's pleasant and comfortable and my thoughts flip between Max and Will. My thoughts of Max make me excited and happy but my thoughts of Will ground me. I don't have much longer before I have to go back.

With all the time available I manage to crochet three octopuses, the first is a small one and a little wonky but the other two are much better. I cannot wait to give them to the girls. I message Mum and Dad to let them know I'm still fine, but I'm not really looking at my phone for their benefit. It's so I don't miss a message from Max.

It makes a noise and I jump.

Message to Anna
We should be back on Sunday for the week, I've managed to confirm my annual leave now which is great, it's been so busy in the office! xx

I try to keep my features neutral as I read the message, aware Dotty is assessing me. I grab another ball of yarn and start on my next crochet square, so therapeutic. I'm making Dotty a blanket now, something that will go with her décor.

She eyes me suspiciously and then changes the subject.

'These are amazing, Anna you really are talented. You could sell these.'

'Really? No one has ever really thought much of it apart from it being a bit silly really.'

'Yes! Have a look online and there's a local market that sells crafts and things like this.'

And with Dotty's encouragement I find a local Facebook group where people show what they've crocheted and others leave comments, there's even some smaller pieces which people hide for the children to find. It's so sweet, I can imagine Neve and Hazel loving finding little treasures like that, a true act of kindness. There are some signposts to people's own personal selling sites. I click on one, there are loads of different things on sale and looking at it and the prices, I'm gobsmacked. I spend the rest of the afternoon researching selling crochet and I'm excited to say the least. I can barely keep my hands and feet still for the rest of the day. Could I sell one of my creations? It looks as though it could be possible. I decide I need to walk this extra energy off and have a real think about it.

I walk around the park, my heart beating fast as I imagine selling my own stuff. Could I really do it? I have tons of bits and pieces at home that I've crocheted over the years. The thought of going to get them brings me back to the inevitable. How much longer can I stay down here before I have to see *him*. And *her*. Are they together now? Laughing at me. My thoughts have taken a sour turn and no matter how much I try to push them away I go over all the times we were together, looking for signs. Was it a full-blown love affair, or was it just once? Did she marry Eddie? How could Eloise do this to me when she's been my friend, my family, for so long? I compare my situation with Max's. It could be worse; he lost his wife.

I miss him and the girls.

Chapter 18

I've taken to hiding a few of my creations around town in small bags to keep them clean and developed an unhealthy obsession with checking the group to see if anyone's found them and posted a message about them. No luck yet, but I'm hopeful. I pop one next to a tree and walk away watching for a few minutes, there's a little boy running around nearby, imagine if I get to see the joy of someone finding one. I walk back over to the path and watch, but although the boy heads towards my tree, he changes direction at the last minute and runs back to his mummy. I just about give up and decide to continue leaving out more creations when a tiny dog bolts to my tree and picks up the bag. Crap. I run after the dog. Considering how small it is, it's fast.

'Here dog, here dog,' I yell. 'It's not for you,' I growl under my breath.

'Who is it for?' a voice behind me asks. 'Here Butch, here Butch.'

The dog runs back to its owner. 'Drop it. Drop

it,' he says sternly. The dog reluctantly obeys his command.

My face flames. How do I explain what I'm doing to a complete stranger? I turn around as the man brings the slightly worse for wear bag containing my still intact crochet creation back to me, a small blue butterfly.

'I believe this is yours.' He hands it to me and as he does so he gives me a curious look. 'Anna?' he questions and I stifle an inward groan. Who now?

I lift my eyes from my sad, soiled bag up to his face and I'm surprised to see Derek. He's older but his features are the same, his hair is still looking good, curly and dark. I thought he was the one, so sweet. So different from the others. Have I landed in some alternate universe where all my old boyfriends have come to live? What the hell is going on?

'You look great, almost didn't recognise you with the hair,' Derek says, interrupting my thoughts. 'Sorry about Butch.' He smiles warmly.

I look down at the tiny dog. 'Butch? Really, that dog doesn't look like a Butch.'

He shrugs in the way he used to, a soft motion, one shouldered and with a sideways grin. 'I love the irony.'

'Hmmm.' I grin. It's good to see him. My last boyfriend before Will, perhaps the one that got away. And here he is.

'How are you? Are you seeing anyone?' he asks, and I shake my head. His grin broadens. 'Nor me.' His eyes shine at me and it brings me back to the breakup. The drawn-out process of breaking up with someone when you really don't want to but you can't get past what they did. Not a betrayal as bad as Will's with Eloise but there were a lot of tears and a lot of pain before I felt ready to move on.

'Are you still writing your poems?' I ask, moving the conversation away from our love lives.

'Not so much now, had to get something to pay the bills but it's still my passion, you know.'

'That's great.' I nod, turning on my heel, thinking that's enough. I don't want to speak with him. The pain's gone now but he's not someone I want in my life now.

'Wait, are you doing these now?' He tries to draw me back in, pointing at the bag in my hand. 'What is that?'

'Just something silly,' I say, feeling self-conscious, not wanting to go into what they are.

He shakes his head, a smile spreading across his face. 'Anna, Anna, it's so good to see you. It's like, why did we ever break up?' He shakes his head at the craziness of it all.

It's like a blow to the chest, the audacity of him speaking those words when he knows why. What kind of reaction is he expecting? The heat in my face deepens.

'You cheated is why and you know that.' I go to turn away again, completely done now, embarrassed, exhausted and fed up.

He sighs, physically and loudly and it's enough to make me turn back.

'I can't believe you're still holding onto that. You

know it wasn't my fault, the guys pushed me into it. I made one mistake in two years and then it was over.'

'One mistake? Sleeping with someone else is a huge betrayal and don't be so weak as to blame it on your friends. Butch is no more butch than you're no more to blame for your own actions.'

'I know but I always thought we got each other in that way?'

'In what way?' I question, exasperated.

'We were both always kind of pushovers.' He lifts his shoulders and it makes my teeth grind.

'Pushovers? You think I'm a pushover?' I demand, but I can't help thinking back over all the times I've said something is okay at the cost of my own feelings. The times I've been pushed into doing things I don't necessarily want to do. All the times Eloise had me acting like her lap dog. I always thought I was happy to do it but really, perhaps she wasn't that great a friend after all. I mean, she slept with my boyfriend so she obviously wasn't a great friend.

A huge sigh escapes my mouth at the realisation. I am a pushover.

'Sorry, you're right,' he says. 'I don't know you anymore. Perhaps you're not that way now. Are you still the best of friends with Eloise?'

'No. Not at all actually,' I say through gritted teeth, trying to stop the tears that have suddenly started springing into my eyes. Don't cry. Don't cry. Not in front of him.

'Oh. Perhaps you aren't a pushover then. I'm

sorry for saying that, Anna. You're right I did a horrible thing and the breakup was hard on me too. I know why we're not together; I don't know why I said that. I just saw you and I guess I felt nostalgic or something, you were a great girlfriend. Even if I wasn't a great boyfriend.'

His kind words soften me. I'm finding it hard to hold onto my anger. I'd dealt with it such a long time ago with him. But I can feel a lump in my throat, I sniff loudly, willing myself to stop but it's too late. A big fat tear falls down my face, betraying me.

'It's not you,' I sob, trying to stop Derek from thinking that his actions from years ago are still so important to me.

He comes close, Butch at his heel jumping up, desperate for his master's attention.

'It's okay, Anna, I feel that way too sometimes.'

His kind words undo me and now my little sobs turn to big, fat ones as I understand where I am and what I'm doing.

'Do you want to talk about it?' he asks, looking uncomfortable. But it's not him I want to talk to. There's only one person who I find myself wishing was here and it makes absolutely no sense because I barely know him.

'No, I'…m… b…being… s…silly.' I manage to get the words out between my erratic breathing.

'You're clearly upset. Perhaps I could help,' he says kindly, placing an unsure hand lightly on my shoulder.

'My …b…boyfriend…ch…cheated…on….me. w.w.with… El..El'

'Eloise?' he ventures, his eyebrows shooting up.

I nod mutely, grateful I don't have to continue speaking.

'That bitch,' he spits.

His arm comes round me and I lean into him, happy for the comfort but uncomfortable with the who. I'd just come here to put some crochet bits out and now I'm a complete mess.

Chapter 19

'Max, you're back. And you girls,' I add, before bending down to Hazel and Neve. I spread my arms wide while they both walk into me, squeezing me tight.

'Yes, we're down for a few weeks now.' He smiles down at me.

I turn my face up to his. 'Oh yes, you said, that's great.' I feel flustered and am praying my rapidly heating cheeks aren't giving me away. Why is this man getting to me? I concentrate to keep my hands from touching my face and giving me away further. *He* may be here for a few weeks but I can't be for much longer.

Dotty watches us with a curious grin on her face, her head going to and fro between us. She's working something out.

'You had a call about the car whilst you were out, Anna. He said you can pick it up tomorrow.'

I turn my attention to Dotty although I'm still acutely aware of Max's presence. I don't know why he's having such an effect on me. Since our text message exchanges, I feel awkward and flustered; he's not just Dotty's moody grandson anymore.

'That's great news,' I trill, but the happiness doesn't reach my voice. There's no reason for me to stay now. It really is time to go back and face them. I'll miss Max, and Dotty and of course the girls too. They're such little treasures.

'You should return the car,' Dotty suggests. 'It will only take a day and then you can come back. I really think it'll be good for you. Some closure.' She nods along with her words encouragingly.

Max looks at me puzzled. 'You have someone else's car?' he asks, a playfulness and amusement in his voice.

'Long story, but perhaps I'll go in a few days.' I still can't face it. I just don't want to head back. I have a bit longer before I have to go back to work. Though I know I'm delaying the inevitable.

'If you're not busy, me and the girls were thinking of going on the steam train today?'

'Wow, that sounds lovely,' I enthuse, turning any thoughts of driving home off. I can spare another day.

'Sounds lovely. Choo choo,' Neve echoes me then starts to choo around the house with Hazel chooing behind her, holding onto her hooded jumper as she follows.

'Are you coming, Granny?' Hazel asks Dotty, batting her long eyelashes and pulling on Dotty's cardigan. 'Please?'

'Oh no dear, I think I need a lie down but you lot

go out, I'm tired today and I've got a friend popping round in about an hour.' She pats Hazel gently on the head and bends down to squish Neve.

'How's she been?' Max asks in hushed tones as we pack up the car.

'Um fine,' I say.

He gives me a puzzled look. 'You carers are real thorough, you know.' He gives me a cheesy grin and I find it hard to push down the lump in my throat. If only he knew. Dotty is going to get me into trouble here.

'Yes, she's seems to be well, just a bit tired today.' I'm wondering why they think she needs such a high level of care. Dotty may be a bit tired today but she's one of the spriteliest people I know. She's old. It's not weird to be tired, I'm not even old and I'm often tired.

'Good, thank you.' He grins. 'It does make me feel better that you're here. I'll stop going on about it now.'

We all hold hands and hop on the train; it's an old steam train so feels a little like we're going to *Hogwarts*. I go to mention it to the girls and realise they're probably not the right audience for that yet.

Neve is potty training and absolutely obsessed with the bathroom, so we spend an extraordinary amount of time going to the toilet. I take turns with Max which he is grateful for having spent most of the morning in the bathroom.

'She's determined that's it now,' he laughs. 'She won't put a nappy on at all. I'm spending a lot of time at bedtime convincing her that her little bladder just isn't ready for through the night yet.'

I smile indulgently at Neve, she's such a little peach and so clever. I'm astounded that someone so little can have such strong opinions already. I fumble in my bag and pull out the little octopuses I crocheted for them. Their little faces light up at the small creations in my hand.

'I've missed you both so much.' I grin as they snuggle into me.

'We've missed you too, and Mummy,' Hazel says.

It's the first time I've heard her say mummy and I'm a little startled.

'Oh, I bet you do,' I say reassuringly, giving her arm a little pat, suddenly feeling choked with emotion at the thought of these girls being motherless.

'Hey, look girls we're almost at the station.' Max points out of the window and the girls leap up to look. We're all peering out when Neve announces she needs a wee again and promptly runs towards the train's toilets. Max runs after her but considering her legs are so much smaller than his, she's quick and closes the door before he has a chance to catch up.

I watch in horror as the door slides closed and hear the dreaded click of Neve locking the door behind her.

'Neve,' Max shouts, the panic evident in his voice. 'Let me in sweetie, open the door.'

'It okay, Dada. I just weeing,' comes a little voice from behind the door.

I take Hazel's hand and lead her over to a clearly

upset Max.

'I hope she can unlock the door because I don't know how we'll get her out otherwise,' he mumbles to me under his breath, trying to keep the conversation out of Hazel's earshot.

'Daddy, why's Neve in the bathroom alone?' she asks, her everlasting curiosity getting the better of her.

'Good question,' he says, attempting a smile but it doesn't reach his eyes. He's trying to be strong for Hazel, like he has had to be for so much of her short life.

'Neve, sweetie, could you open the door please.' I use my sweetest sing-song voice to try to encourage her to open the door.

'I did a poo, Daddy,' she shouts proudly, from behind the door.

'That's great, honey. Could you open the door now, then you can show us.'

I could almost laugh if I wasn't so worried about Neve.

'Okay,' she says, and we hear her approach the door fiddling around with the lock.

'Can you open it, sweetie?' Max repeats after a few minutes of hearing her scratch at the door but not the click we're all on high alert for.

'It won't open,' she finally bursts out, and we can hear the tears in her voice. 'Daddy, open the door,' she wails, and it's clear it's beginning to dawn on Neve that she's stuck.

'Daddy, why can't Neve open the door?' Hazel looks between us inquisitively.

I see Max tense; he's already stressed and Hazel's questioning isn't helping.

'Let's go and find the nice man who takes the tickets?' I take Hazel's hand and lead her away in search of help but also so that Max can concentrate on the task in hand and try to keep Neve calm. If she calms down, she may be able to reopen the toilet or hopefully the ticket man can do it.

We've pulled up to the station and the ticket man is asking everyone to get off the train. I go straight over to him.

'Please help, there's a little girl and she's accidently locked herself in the toilets.'

The ticket man harrumphs, clearly put out by my request but he follows us back to Neve and Max.

'What's happened here? Children shouldn't be in the toilets unaccompanied,' he says in a loud, booming voice as he squeezes his large body into the crowded space.

'I know that,' Max says, through gritted teeth. 'She ran into the toilet and locked it before I had a chance to get there, now is there any way for us to get this door open please?'

The ticket man gives an audible sigh displaying his contempt for the situation.

'Hmm. I'm not sure. This has never happened to me before. She locked it can she not get herself back out?'

'She's two-and-a half years old and she locked herself in the loo. She can't open it and as you can hear she's getting a bit distressed now.'

Neve wails in the background scratching at the

door and calling for Daddy.

'It's okay Neve, Daddy is here and I'm not going anywhere. The ticket man has come to help us get you out,' he says, side-eyeing the miserable ticket man.

'I'll go and see if the driver knows what to do,' he mutters, and wanders off.

'Some help he is,' Max grumbles, placing his head in his hands.

'Do you think we could pry it open with a knife of something?' I'm grasping at straws hoping to be helpful at this stressful time. 'I'll take Hazel and we'll go and see if we can get something from the food carriage.' I take her little hand in mine and she walks quietly behind me.

'Are you okay, Hazel?' I ask, when we're out of earshot of Max. I don't think I've ever heard her be so quiet.

She nods solemnly. 'Will Neve ever get out of the toilet?' she asks.

'Of course, she will.' I pat her hand reassuringly. 'It's just finding the best way to do it.'

'I hope it doesn't take too long because I need a wee.' I see the tears welling in her eyes.

'Aww, Hazel. That's no problem, there must be some other toilets, let's pop to them then get the knife.' I take her hand gently and guide her to the next carriage and we find a loo to go in. Poor little darling didn't want to bother everyone that she was bursting for a wee, it's a huge one too and she insists we don't lock the door. I wonder whether after this she'll ever want to use a lock again.

Afterwards we head back to the food carriage and discover that the knives are plastic, so no good, before walking swiftly back to Max.

The not so jolly ticket man is back and he has a screwdriver which he is poking at the lock with.

'Get her to stand back,' he says gruffly to Max.

'Okay, but be careful she's only little,' Max grumbles back, softening his tone as he speaks with Neve. 'Stand away from the door, sweetie. We're just trying to open it.'

'I did a poo,' comes a muffled cry from behind the door.

'I know, that's great. Just stand over near the toilet for a moment.'

After a lot of shimmying and what feels like a lifetime the lock makes the clicking sound. It feels like the best sound in the world as the door slides open and we see Neve cowering next to the toilet.

The ticket man steps in first, looking stern but using a kinder voice with a clearly terrified two-year-old behind the door.

'Now young lady don't lock that door again,' he says, stepping further in to allow Max through. Max scoops her up into his arms and holds Neve while she wraps her tiny arms tightly around his neck like a little koala.

The ticket man turns to us. 'Make sure you stay with her next time,' he growls, the judgement thick in his voice. He sniffs into the air with his huge hairy nostrils and looks down at his feet. In all the commotion he didn't notice as he stepped in but on the bottom of his shoe is a poo... Neve's poo.

'I did a poo, Daddy,' Neve says again.

Max nods, stifling a laugh as it dawns on the ticket man that the brown stink he has just trodden in is actually a human poo.

'Thank you for your help,' Max trills, a lightness to his voice and we hop off the train and decide to take Neve to the café toilets to check her over and clean her up. Luckily Max had a change of clothes for her, so a fresh pair of trousers and knickers later we're ready for the day.

'I think we all deserve an ice cream after that adventure.' Max smiles, the relief evident in his voice.

'Yay!' sing the girls, and I find myself singing it too, so elated that everyone is okay.

Chapter 20

Today's the day, the day I need to get Will's car and go and deal with my ex and my best friend. I've put it off long enough. Perhaps too long.

I told Max yesterday that I needed to go back home to sort a few things out, he encouraged me to go because he's around to look after Dotty.

After the panic of Neve getting trapped in the train toilets, the rest of the day went relatively smoothly. The girls were happy and settled, Neve didn't go to the toilet without an adult present and we all ate lots of yummy treats, sang silly songs and generally enjoyed each other's company. The grumpy poo-shoed ticket man was also fortunately not on the train on the way home, so it was a relief not to have to speak with him again. I almost felt sorry for him having to clean himself up but then I reminded myself how rude and unhelpful he had been in what was a parent's nightmare. We've had a few more fun-filled days out since.

'Hello dear.' Dotty pops down a cup of tea and I

smile up at her. I'm going to miss her when I go back home. I gulp down the tea, savouring the taste and the feeling that goes along with it.

'Thanks, Dotty, you've been amazing,' I start, but I feel it catch in my throat and I busy my hands in my attempt not to cry.

Nothing escapes her notice and she pats my quivering hands.

'You need to go and sort this out so you can move on properly and start afresh.'

I nod along, knowing her words are true but they're not making the thought of doing it any easier.

'I know, I'm going to pick the car up in about half an hour.'

'Okay, well Max and the girls are already out, they should be back soon then you can say goodbye before you're off?'

I nod and go upstairs to pack my belongings. I can't stay here forever, I'm running out of money for a start, even if one of Dotty's friends has offered me some money to make a crocheted blanket for her. It'll tide me over but not for long. I think sadly over everything I've managed to achieve over the last few weeks. I'll be going back to work soon and then I won't have so much time to be creative. Thinking of being back behind the huge marble desk and greeting everyone coming into the hotel fills me with dread. The bigger thought of seeing Eloise swanning around the office makes it even worse.

As I finish packing up my belongings Max enters the room, he comes over to me gently and brings me in for a hug.

'I'm not normally the soppy sort,' he croaks, uncomfortably. 'But I'm so glad that my Gran hired you. You've been like a breath of fresh air to me and the kids. When will you be back?'

It dawns on me that Dotty's innocent lie when we first met still sits between us. He knows I'm going home to sort something out but he doesn't know I'm not a carer and that this isn't my career.

'I'm not a hundred percent sure yet.' My eyes fill but I ignore it and Max folds me into his arms further. I breathe in his scent, letting my body relax into his and turn my face up towards him. He lowers his face down to mine and as our lips finally meet, we share the slowest, most tender kiss. My entire body tingles, enjoying the sensation until I feel my face heats up with emotion. There's so much promise in his kiss but it's all based on a lie. Just as the thought crosses my mind, a stray tear slides down my cheek and I quickly use the back of my hand to wipe it away.

'I really like you,' he says, as he pulls back, his cheeks rosy too and I try my best not to swoon further. 'When you're back I want to take you out. A real date or something.' He grins a silly grin and despite this being bitter sweet, I can't help smiling back at him.

I drive back, taking the same route that I drove over two weeks ago and I find myself reflecting on everything that has happened. I cringe at the kiss-mishap with Joe and also seeing so many of my ex-boyfriends. But I now feel empowered. I'm ready to go and speak with Will. I'm ready to hear what's happened and not sit and blame myself any longer. I need to hear the full story. I need to understand what happened at the wedding if I'm ever going to move forward.

It's a warm day and I pull into the same services that I stopped at on my journey down, to put the hood down before I complete the rest of my journey. I think back to the sad girl of two weeks ago who stopped here in her too-tight bridesmaid dress and bought the psychedelic towel that I'm become strangely fond of. I don't go into the service shops.

I feel so rested I could drive for hours and I enjoy the exhilaration of having the wind in my hair as I drive back home. Or what was my home. There are certainly things to sort out before I can move on.

By the time I get to what was mine and Will's home, I've rehearsed what I'm going to say several times and feel confident and ready to face him and unpick our lives. I take out my keys and head to the front door, patting my little Micra as I pass it on the drive. It may shake on the motorway but it costs nowhere near as much to run as Will's gas-guzzler. I'm looking forward to having my little run-around back.

'Will', I call out, as I come through the door like so many times before, alerting him that I'm home. Was Eloise ever hiding in the cupboards? Perhaps if I'd never called out it would all have been revealed sooner.

'Will?' I call again, louder, but there's no response. I walk through the home that was ours, touching the memories of our past. Nothing has changed since I've been gone, everything is still in the same places. It's only really telling in the bedroom and the kitchen where an assortment of plates and clothes are laid around that show he has been here. But where is he now? He loves to work from home if he can, unless he has some important meetings.

I feel somewhat deflated, I'd pumped myself up ready to say my piece. Instead, I take a bag and begin to pack my belongings. I may not know exactly where I'm going but I'm not staying here. Thoughts of going back to Dotty's flood my brain, but I can't go back yet, I need to deal with everything first. It takes me over an hour to pack up all my clothes.

The house feels incredibly cold, what I once considered my sanctuary feels so disconnected from me. Will is still not home and I debate sitting and waiting in the living room. But then I take a deep breath and decide it's time to go and see Eloise, if she's there. She could, should, still be on her honeymoon.

As I drive onto Eloise and Eddie's huge driveway, I wonder whether Eloise is even still living here? I remember Eddie's face; he was as much in the dark as I was. But this is the only place I know where to start, at least Eddie should be able to tell me what's happened.

I knock on the door and all the bravado I'd found on the way here is suddenly lost. Do I really want to know? What if Will is here? I force my hand to knock a bit louder and hear shuffling behind the door. I inhale deeply readying myself to face the music.

Chapter 21

I lose my nerve and turn to walk away; I can't do it. I can't face Eloise. Not now. It's official, I'm a coward, I'm defeated. Standing up to a few old boyfriends doesn't mean I'm ready for this. All the feelings come flooding back, second best again. Second best always. She's probably not here anyway.

What am I thinking? It all swirls around in my head. Eloise. She can do no wrong. Eloise is beautiful and not in an unconventional way but in an obvious, in your face, way and everyone sees it. Eloise is clever, she's accomplished so much and so young. She dresses well, she looks great, she's tiny without too much effort. Everyone falls at her feet and I realise that included me. I'm almost back to my car, after practically running the length of their huge driveway when I hear a shaky voice. It's her. I've never heard her voice like that before.

'Anna?' she calls again, a little less croaky but not like her, unsure.

I can't help it, I'm curious. I turn to look at her and she suddenly doesn't look so wonderful anymore. Okay, she has lost weight (that she didn't need to) for the wedding but she's skinnier, almost gaunt and she's pale, her golden glow gone. I stare at her with my mouth hanging open unashamedly. She stands hunched, smaller.

'Anna,' her voice is soft and quieter than normal, I almost have to strain to hear it. 'I've been hoping you'd come. Come in, let's talk.' It's more of a question than a command and I look longingly at my car.

I could just get in it and leave because I don't owe her a thing, but I can't help but wonder. Curiosity killed the cat they say, let's hope it doesn't do the same to me.

I step over the familiar threshold ignoring the grandeur of her beautifully decorated house. Eloise was always messing with it; it'd be a little different every time I came, like a continuous spot the difference. She'd decorate and re-decorate and each time it would look more and more impressive, more expensive, styled to suit the times, the latest fashions and trends, a beautiful antique find, a suggestion from a friend. She was never satisfied, that feeling extended beyond the house.

I sit mutely on her sofa; we've shared so many memories here, drunk loads of bottles of wine, as a twosome, as a foursome, within a big dinner party. I cross my legs awkwardly, focusing on my shoes, my flat comfortable shoes; she must be hating that I didn't take my shoes off. I uncross my legs and put

150

both feet on the carpet. Almost smiling to myself. Petty but so satisfying.

'You look well, I love your hair,' she says conversationally, her tone returning to a more normal voice now she's got me in here. She's back in her position of power. She settles a glass of water in front of me, no tea. I don't intend to stay long.

I let the silence sit between us, knowing it'll be making her squirm. Trying to shift the power dynamics, I look pointedly at her mint green tracksuit, it's a perfect fit but not what she would usually be seen in or let anyone see her in, even me.

I'm not here to make small talk but now I'm here I don't know where to start. My mouth is so dry and I move my tongue around to moisten it, willing myself to ask the difficult question. The question I've pushed away and aside and yet it's still hanging over me. I slurp at my glass of water, stalling for time. I need to do this, so I can move on. Do it. Do it, Anna. Now.

'When?' It comes out louder than I intended, giving away my nerves. Damn.

'You really want to know?' she asks, shuffling around in her seat.

'Yes,' I say plainly, willing my voice not to shake; I don't want her to see the pain she's caused.

'He came on to me, you know, he started it. He'd been pursuing me for ages. When I introduced him to you it all stopped for a while of course, but then I got a bit too drunk one evening and Eddie was being such a beast, you know what he's like and it just happened.' It comes out quickly and her confidence returns as she regales me with the details. Like it's the latest gossip about a shared friend or acquaintance. There's almost a smirk on her face, is she enjoying this now? She flicks her hand away like it's so irrelevant and I see the ring on her finger, an expensive golden band.

I take a gulp to clear my throat and force myself to press on, not wanting to get into what happened at the wedding following my very public exit, just yet.

'How long did it go on for?' My voice comes out flat and almost robotic, going through the motions now.

'Well, once it started it became hard to stop.' She falters, searching for the words. 'When someone adores you so much it's hard not to enjoy that, I guess, and Eddie was so busy with work and wasn't paying much attention to me. I was so stressed with the wedding. I mean, you know, I did everything.' She looks down at her hands, fiddles with her ring.

'Hmmm,' I respond, what does she want me to do, absolve her of what she's done?

'I kept trying to get him to leave me alone, but he was so persistent. I thought it would stop after the wedding and everything would go back to normal. A momentary blip, a touch of cold feet and then me and Eddie would enter into married bliss with the two of you back on track too.'

Is she trying to sell it to me as though it didn't matter they were having an affair, because they intended to stop? I suck my lips in to prevent my mouth from hanging open at her audacity.

'So, it's okay because you were going to stop?' I ask boldly.

'No, that's not what I said, you're putting words into my mouth now. I only meant you were never meant to find out.'

'Oh, that's okay then.' I let the sarcasm drip from my words, and I see Eloise visibly pull back.

'No, that's not what I meant either.' She huffs. 'It's hard to explain, I didn't mean for everything to get out of hand, he was just so persistent, I shouldn't have but it was so hard to say no.'

'You're making it so much better.' I chortle, shaking my head.

'You're misunderstanding me,' she tries again. Oh poor Eloise the victim of her best friend's boyfriend trying to sleep with her.

'I think it's quite the opposite, actually, I understand you perfectly.' I get up to leave and she stands in front of me.

'What does that mean? I made a mistake. I'm sorry, okay? Surely, we can salvage our friendship. You're practically a sister to me, you lived in my house when we were growing up. I miss you.' The tears are running freely down her face, but I don't buy them. Crocodile tears, she's only sorry she got caught.

'There's no friendship here to salvage now, you ruined that when you slept with my boyfriend, not once, but repeatedly. I don't owe you anything and the fact you would throw our childhood in my face shows how you don't know me at all. I don't know how Eddie forgave you. Perhaps he's a bigger person than I am, but you don't deserve him and you don't deserve me.'

As if he's been summoned, I hear a loud slam from the front door and Eddie walks into the room. His face is like thunder and I wonder if he's about to shout at me, but his anger isn't directed towards me. The red is creeping up from his neck to his face and ears, he looks as though he could blow at any moment.

When he finally opens his mouth a growly snarl comes out. 'I thought I told you to be out by now.'

Eloise looks shaken and I almost feel sorry for her.

'And take the goddamn ring off, it's embarrassing. I don't know why I married you that day, maybe it was to save face, but I cannot wait for the annulment. Now get out and take your friend with you.'

When he says friend he looks right at me, before doing a double take and realising who I am.

'Anna?' he questions, his tone softening but the redness on his cheeks remaining.

'Yes.' I smile at my friend, the only one in the room I would consider a friend now.

Eloise turns and leaves, presumably to get her stuff together. I look around the living room, now noticing some of her things missing. Eddie comes over to me, taking me in his big, bear-like arms.

'It's good to see you.' He grins. 'Where have you been? And you look great.' He looks me up and down when he says this, resting his eyes on my hair.

'Thank you.' I've almost resorted back to my

schoolgirl self. Eddie is incredibly handsome, and he smells divine.

'I went away for a few weeks to clear my head,' I explain and I find myself offloading the adventures of the last two weeks on him. Explaining everything that happened between myself and Max. The more I talk about him the more flustered I feel, my thoughts frequently returning to *that* kiss. I'll admit I miss him and those cheeky girls.

'So, what happened at the wedding?' I ask. The final question falling from my lips.

Chapter 22

Eddie busies himself making me a cup of coffee. It's a far cry from Dotty's builders' tea but it's needed. I shake my head at it all. It's surreal being in what was Eddie and Eloise's house but without Eloise. After a few slammed doors and stomping around, which Eddie and I dutifully ignored, she slipped quietly out of the front door about half an hour ago.

'I've still not decided fully if I'm going to take her back, but I want her to sweat and have a think about what she did. She humiliated me on our wedding day.' Eddie places my cup in front of me as I sit at the vast island in their expensive kitchen.

'It sounds awful,' I soothe, realising that while we're experiencing a similar pain, his is worse. He had everyone he loved at that wedding to witness what unfolded. 'I still can't believe you went ahead with it.' I try to keep my face neutral and non-judgemental but it seems so unlike Eddie to stand for it.

'No one at the wedding knew the full story,

although there were questions when you left and then Will was sent packing but we could spin it was just him and his feelings.' He looks up at me sheepishly.

'It's okay, it was a shitty situation. I don't know how I would have handled being in your shoes.' Eloise was always good at putting a spin on things too, that's why they were such a good match.

'I think I was so shell shocked I hadn't fully computed what had happened. I think the rational part of me wanted to get through the day, save face and pretend like it didn't happen or it was a one off but it wasn't. We even went on the honeymoon, but we came back early, and I just couldn't do it. I thought we might get through it; the honeymoon was a good distraction, she was trying so hard, sweet and attentive the whole time but I could barely let her touch me. The honeymoon was okay, nowhere near as good as it should have been. There's only so long someone can be on their best behaviour. Then when we got back here, I started looking at the rooms and wondering. Did it happen in here, did they sleep in my sheets, when did it happen because I sure as hell didn't notice anything amiss. Did you?' He appraises me checking he hasn't been betrayed again, all that trust out the window.

'I had no idea until Will stood up and even then I thought it was a messed-up prank. I even thought you were in on it.' I take a big sip of my coffee bringing myself back into the room and out of the memory of that horrible day.

'Sorry, of course you didn't know. Anyway, it

started driving me crazy and I couldn't bear it. I was quizzing her constantly, getting her to tell me all the details, exactly when, exactly how. I thought if I knew everything, I could forget about it but it just made it worse. Things have been very strained; I still don't know what I'll do but I need some space from her so I asked her to pack up and move out for a bit. Let me clear my head and give me the space to work out what I want. She was supposed to be out by the time I got home. We had a blazing row this morning because she thought I should move out; can you believe her? I just don't know if I could ever trust her again, Anna. What do you think? The only problem is I still love her.' He places his head in his hands, trying to contain his emotions.

I lift my shoulders up in response. 'I can't answer that for you,' I say simply, that is not my decision and his capacity to forgive is within him not me.

'Have you forgiven her?' he asks softly, bringing his brown eyes to meet mine.

I shoulder shrug again. 'Not yet, I don't think we'll ever be close again. It's all too raw to say yet,' I say noncommittally. I don't want Eddie making his decisions based on what I'm doing.

'I just keep thinking of all those times we went holidaying together; were they sneaking off the whole time?' He pushes his hand through his hair, there are large dark circles under his eyes and I can see the strain the situation has taken on him. He's normally so well-groomed and composed. A perfect match for Eloise.

'I don't know,' I admit, but there's still someone

who can give me the answers.

'Eloise says they weren't but I don't know what to believe, even as I made her sit down and go over the whole sorry affair, bit by bit. She kept changing her story or getting muddled so it didn't instill much confidence. What did Will say?'

'I haven't spoken to him yet,' I mumble, but I know he hears me because his eyebrows shoot up into his hairline.

'Don't you want to know?' he asks. 'It's killing me, but I need to know everything, I've spent hours going through every interaction they ever had in my head and it still doesn't make sense. I just didn't see it or think they would do that to me, to us. How can I ever trust someone again?'

'Oh, believe me it's been on my mind even if I haven't been questioning Will about it. Has he tried to contact you?'

'Yes, he has, the arsehole. But I'm not interested, and I hope he doesn't think he's going to get any of my business now. I won't be dealing with him again. Our friendship, and any other affiliation, is over. She was going to be my wife and according to her he pursued her but I'm not so sure about it all really. She's a strong woman and she could have said no, she could have told me, she could have told you. She knew what she was doing no matter how much she wants to play the victim. Once may be a mistake but an affair? That's a betrayal.' He spits the last few words out as if they taste bad in his mouth.

I nod my agreement, feeling the force of Eddie's anger and also relief that I'm not facing that. I certainly wouldn't want to be in Eloise's shoes but I'm not a cheat.

Chapter 23

I force myself to go back to what was mine and Will's home, half hoping he won't be there. I'm exhausted from talking to Eloise and Eddie but I know I can't move on fully until I have this out with Will. When I get back there's another car on the drive, I have no idea who it belongs to but it doesn't feel great. Is this another girl's car? Another girl he was pursuing into an affair? My stomach flips as I slowly unlock the door and push it open.

'So, there you are. I was wondering when I would see you. Thanks for returning my car, by the way what happened to the upholstery?' His face is set in a twisted sneer.

I wasn't expecting a welcoming home party but his contempt for me is palpable. What did I do? Okay I took his car but that was his own fault. The anger begins to rise in me as he watches me, the sneer still on his face.

'It got wet,' I say, stating the obvious and adding a nonchalant shrug. Who cares it's just a car, it's nothing compared to what he's done.

'Did you do that because of the Eloise thing? I didn't have you pegged as *that* kind of girl,' he spits the words at me, words that drip with disdain. Who is this stranger?

'What kind of girl?' I match his tone; I'm not apologising for the car.

'Petty and vindictive. Feel good, did it? Ruining my car.' Still the sneer stays.

'I had it repaired for fuck's sake, Will, get over yourself. I couldn't work out how to close the sunroof and it rained. Perhaps if you had ever let me drive it, I would have known how it works.'

'So, you're just stupid then too.' He tuts.

'I must have been,' I practically yell. 'For being with you. So shut up you vindictive, spiteful, little man. You are the root cause of so many people's unhappiness and I don't deserve your attitude or nastiness. You should have ended it with me. Although Eloise didn't choose you either, I see.' Almost smirking now, I fold my arms across my chest, it feels good to get it out, to let him know what I think.

'No, she was too chicken shit but she wanted to. She'll come crawling back; they always do. Just wait and see.'

I stare at this stranger in front of me, the cruelty in his voice shocks me. Did I ever even know this man? Yes, he could be impatient at times, I'd find his fingers drumming on the table whilst he waited for his food. It was irritating but I just thought he was hangry. This is something else. This is something deeper, something nasty.

'Since when did you become such a nasty bastard?'

'Since when did you become some hippy chick, what happened to your hair and clothes?' My hand immediately goes to the cut I had done a few weeks ago. I still love it and the colour, it's not something Will would like but who cares what he likes.

'Fuck off, Will. You're a cheating scumbag. For future reference, don't start something with someone if you're interested in someone else. Don't start something with someone before you have finished it with someone else. And don't be a complete arsehole about it all when it all comes out,' I shout the last few words as the fury bursts out of me, all the while watching his snarling face.

'Fuck off, Anna. It was never going anywhere with us anyway.'

'News to me.' I feel the full force of his comments pressing down on my chest. How can he be so dismissive?

'Really?' He rolls his uncaring eyes; there's a cruel edge to him and it makes me want to shrink away before anything more hurtful spills from his lips.

Instead, I bring myself up to my full height, it's nowhere near as tall as Will but it helps me to feel strong, standing tall.

'Why did you do it? We were living together; we had a life together.' The words come out small and quiet and I kick myself for seeming as though I care but I do, I can't deny it. The tears form in my eyes and I blink them back. I need to hold tight.

'Ah so you want all the gory details, do you? I always liked Eloise but she was with Eddie and then she set me up with you and she was so excited about it. When I met you, you were a duller version of her and I thought, okay. But it was really what being with you did to Eloise that made it worth it. The more attention I paid to you, the more it drove her wild and before I knew it, we were having an affair.'

A stray tear escapes, betraying me. The cruelty of it all hits me, he used me the whole time. The whole damn time.

'Did you ever have feelings for me?' I ask, the tears running freely.

He softens a little. 'Of course, I did. For a while nothing happened with Eloise, and I did try to focus on you. My family loves you and you were always good in any work or social situation. I thought perhaps I would forget about her especially when you moved in, but I loved her, it's not my fault.'

'Great, thanks for trying.' I roll my eyes at him; he makes me sound like such an acceptable substitute. Arsehole.

'Then Eddie and Eloise got engaged and started planning their wedding and we were chatting one time about the future. I don't know where you and Eddie were but it suddenly happened. Like the idea that she and I would both officially be off the market really got her going.' He smirks again.

I stop him by holding my hands up. 'I don't want to hear you reminiscing about your failed affair. I've cancelled all the bills so you can go sort that shit out yourself,' I inform him. I'm done, I don't need all the sordid details like Eddie, I know what they did now. I know it was them both. Cheats, the pair of them, who deserve each other.

I go around the house packing my stuff into bags. Will stays hot on my heels making the occasional comment but I think mainly to check I don't take any of his crap, not that I'd want any of that shit.

I get all my crochet stuff out and begin to pack it into my bags.

'Taking all that crap, are you? You should get some cats then you can be a proper old spinster,' he taunts.

I don't answer, my tears have dried and I work robotically, methodically pulling our lives apart.

I hate this cruel version of him and wondering if I missed this all or if it's just the embarrassment. Perhaps I've had a lucky escape after all. He was always a sore loser; he'd mope and moan about the football if it didn't go his way. I remember once I thought something really bad had happened as he stomped into the kitchen and slammed around, his fists clenched but no, it was just that his fantasy football team was sliding down the fantasy table. It took hours for his mood to calm down and, as was usual when he had moods like this over nothing, I'd generally avoid him, accepting this as a part of him. Allowing it to be okay. Most of the time he was charming and kind, so did it really matter that he had these moments? No one is perfect. But he was far worse than I thought, a liar, a cheat and I remind myself of that as I bring the last few bits of my stuff through the living room and leave them at the front door. I stand there for a few minutes, gathering myself. This is it. Our chapter closed.

'Bye then,' he singsongs in a sneery voice.

I turn slowly and with purpose, I imagine my face is bright red as I can feel the heat burning my cheeks.

'You're a liar, a cheat and an arsehole. Look what you did and you still didn't get what you wanted. I hope you learn from this, you smug wanker. Turn yourself around otherwise you'll be the one who ends up alone. Not me. You're pathetic and I feel sorry for you.'

As I turn on my heel, I hear him spluttering to answer but I don't want to hear his witty retort or speak with him any further. I'm done. I walk to the car, load the last boxes up quickly and get in. The tears begin near the end of the street, falling full and heavy, all the pain pouring out. Everything I've tried to forget and to push away has finally come to the surface and I feel the full force of grief for the life I thought we would have together. The tears are beginning to blur my vision and I know I can't drive back to the coast. There's only one place to go now, and it's well overdue a visit.

Chapter 24

I drive down the familiar street, indicate left and follow the road down the little lane to the last few houses in the cul-de-sac. I visited this house regularly, lived there my whole childhood but I never felt very at home. I was so busy coveting Eloise and her family's life whilst my parents worked endlessly to provide for me.

I swallow hard, it's been a difficult time reflecting on myself and my behaviours, but I realise, guiltily, that I've kept them at arm's length for a long time almost considering Eloise's family more of a family to me than my own. My parents aren't perfect, but I don't think I gave them their fair dues. They were ready, willing even, to look after me when my life fell apart in a humiliating way and yet again, I pushed them away. That must have hurt them, not allowing them to be there for me. I wipe at my eyes trying to still the flow of tears, not wanting my parents to see me like this. My thoughts flit to Max and the girls and how he works so hard to fulfil everything for them, but he must be away a lot in the week and without a mother that must be incredibly hard for all of them too.

I pull into the driveway and Mum's out of the door before I can unbuckle my seat belt. She pulls me into a slightly awkward hug. I realise that before this happened, I would have assumed she was just going through the motions, something she thought she was meant to do, she's never really been a big hugger. But there are tears in her eyes and the way she squeezes me makes me think I've got her all wrong. I've misjudged her. And Dad.

'We've been so worried. I'm so happy to see you,' she mumbles in my ear.

Dad comes out and stands beside her, carefully putting his hand on her shoulder in what I would have seen as an uncomfortable move but now I see as solidarity.

'I'm happy to see you too,' I say, the words falling haphazardly out of my mouth, the sentiment is there though.

'I'm sorry I've not been in touch much.' I feel like a bad daughter.

Dad raises his hand in protest. 'We understand, love. It's been a really difficult time. Did you do something to your hair?'

Mum swats away the silly question, rolling her eyes at me conspiratorially. 'Of course she has, it looks great.'

'I'm going to make us all some tea, do you want some?' Dad gestures for me to come through to the kitchen.

I nod, trying to stop the millionth tear pouring from my eyes but this time it's happiness. I finally feel like we are a little family.

I sit on our old-fashioned sofas, and I tell them about everything that happened, even the hard bits. They don't interrupt me or question me but sit quietly and listen, taking it all in. In the past I would have taken their lack of questions as a sign of disinterest and it would have driven me mad, made me think they didn't care. But now, as I look at their tired faces, I realise they do care, they're listeners. That's all it was. Eloise's family was loud, bustling, and always talking over one another. I thought it was interest and excitement, but now I see it for what it was; they were trying to outshine one another. Showing off, shouting louder so their voice was heard. A family of high achievers not listening, not waiting for their turn to talk. There may have been quieter moments in my house and the silence really did drive me mad, but I was heard. I was always heard. After all these years, thinking they didn't care, I finally see them for what they are and the strength they have. My parents may not be the most well-dressed or confident or outspoken but they do have the ability to listen and that should not be underestimated or unappreciated. After all, everyone wants to be heard, even Eloise. Especially Eloise.

I stay overnight and we spend the next day chatting and milling around the house in companiable quiet and I feel more comfortable here than I have in a long time. It's weird to be back in my childhood bedroom but I've never enjoyed my parents' company so much. After the emotional toll of the day before I couldn't bring myself to drive back to the coast, if that *is* what I should be doing. I just don't know. I *want* to go back, to slot back into the life I was building at Dotty's, but it's not my real life.

I'm lost. I've come back here and given Will's car back, my holiday from work is almost over and now I feel myself deflate at the thought of returning to my life, the stares, the pity that I will have to endure all whilst working in the same company as Eloise. Everyone saw, everyone probably knows what happened.

I think back to the horrible day that changed everything and what everyone saw. They saw Will stand up and humiliate me and they saw us all rush off and me rush out and then somehow in the midst of that Eloise and Eddie got married. Most likely everyone thinks it's all Will, that Eloise was an innocent victim. That's the part she's playing, putting a spin on it. She would say that you can spin anything you want. I used to find it endearing, her ability to spin things, thinking it was her trying to get the good out of everything, a positive attribute, but it really wasn't. How blind was I not to see? She spun things to her advantage again and again and I accepted it like the sheep that I was.

How will I face her or anyone at work? I feel physically sick even thinking about it. I can't bear the idea. I suppose I could set the record straight, tell everyone what really happened. That idea doesn't fill me with joy either. Perhaps I would have a short-lived thrill whilst everyone saw Eloise for who she really is but putting someone down isn't how I would like to live my life. And really her job is all Eloise has now because I don't think Eddie will take her back; he's far too hurt and angry.

I sit at the dining room table; Mum's busying herself cleaning the already clean house and I look up at her.

'All alright, dear?' she asks.

I nod but then I shake my head. Why pretend? 'Not really, I'm dreading going back to work.'

She purses her lips. 'I bet.' She holds the silence allowing me the space to think.

'I don't want to go back at all.' It feels good to say it. It may not be a possibility but it's nice to unburden myself. Honestly, it's not the first time I've felt like it. It's not a job that makes my heart sing but it's tolerable, it paid the bills and one of the perks was being with Eloise, being able to go out for long lunches with her, gossiping about what was going on with the hotel, but now…

'Perhaps you shouldn't,' she offers, interrupting my train of thought.

'I don't really think that's an option.'

'Why not?' Her pale eyes daring me to challenge her, my sensible mother with a fire in her belly.

'Well, I need money for a start and I'll need to get a place and start over.' It all feels rather grim to say. Start over my life. Back to the start, don't pass go, don't collect two-hundred pounds. The game of *Monopoly* wins.

'Me and your Dad have some money we would

like to give you,' she says earnestly.

'Don't be silly that's your nest egg.'

'It's not our nest egg we're giving you, it's some other money. We may not be flush like other families, but we've saved up over time. We've been careful and clever with our money; it won't be long and we'll retire early and really get the benefit of it but we always saved a little for you too. We were looking for the right time to give it to you and I think that's now.'

I feel the well of tears begin to brim again. I'm choked up by their kindness and consideration, we may not have had so many fancy holidays, but they can retire early and they have some money for me.

'So, what will you do?' she asks.

I shrug. 'I should go back though, that would be the sensible thing to do.' I appeal to the side I'm used to seeing, her practical side.

'Sensible is overrated.' She shakes her head, her hair swishing to and fro. 'Life is for living, I don't regret anything but if I did it all again, I don't think I would be so sensible, and I've never thought that job suited you.'

I'm intrigued now. 'What job do you think would suit me?'

'Well, I always saw you as a creative really, I thought you'd do something in that space. You always loved your crochet and various crafts and you were wonderful at art at school. And living down on the coast obviously agrees with you, I've never seen you look so good. You shine,' she says *shine* a little shyly, uncomfortable with the term.

'What makes you shine, Mum?' I giggle, deflecting the conversation and almost enjoying her obvious awkwardness.

'Oh, shut up you,' she says affectionately, swatting at me. 'That job doesn't suit you though, does it?'

I ponder her words, she's right, it's not really a job I would have chosen for myself but equally I never had a real clue what I wanted to do. Yes, I knew the creative things that I liked but what to do with them was another question altogether. Could I really make money out of them?

I make a rash decision and message my manager.

Hi Jane, don't be mad with me but I'm not coming back. I have another few weeks of holiday this year I've not taken, consider this my notice. Do I need to come back into the hotel at all? Anna x

Hi Anna, with your leave I don't think you need to come into the office although I would love to see you so I'm happy to meet for a drink or lunch elsewhere and if you want to go over anything with your final pay let me know. Jane x

Later on, I get a message from Eloise

Message to Anna
Really, you don't have to quit.

Message to Eloise
It doesn't have anything to do with you.

She can take that remark any way she likes. She'll probably put a positive spin on it. But she can't resist getting the last word in.

Message to Anna
Oh, I think it has everything to do with me.

Message to Eloise
My decisions are none of your concern now.

And I block her. Finally, I have the last word. I breathe out slowly. It's over. We're done. Goodbye to the cheats.

I sit on my bed contemplating my options, could I go down to the coast? I absentmindedly pick up my phone scrolling to Max's messages and read through our steady stream of messages, I wonder what he's up to right now. A small thrill rises in my chest when I see a new notification that Max has messaged me, until I read it.

Message to Anna
Dotty's in the hospital, thought you should know. Max

I barely even hesitate, I put down my cup of builders' tea on the kitchen table. Yes, that's how I like it now.

Mum looks up, her eyebrows creasing. 'Is everything alright love?'

'I need to go back to the coast; my friend is in hospital.'

Mum looks startled. 'Yes, you must, I do hope

she's okay.'

Mum sets about helping me pack, she makes me a packed lunch and drink whilst Dad goes out to check the car is ready for the journey.

Mum loops her arm with mine as we walk out to the car.

'I know it's early days and you'll want to take it slow,' Mum says warmly. 'But I do like the sound of this Max.'

I grin at her, crushing her and Dad into a hug on the driveway. I'll miss them.

'Me too, Mum, me too.'

Chapter 25

It doesn't take me long to get back to the coast. Without a bathroom break and the traffic being surprisingly kind, I'm back in the familiar town within two hours, a far cry from the first time I came. I've almost driven to Dotty's when I realise she won't be there, my breath catches as I remember, she's in hospital.

A rabble of butterflies is fighting in my stomach, a mixture of concern for Dotty and the thought of seeing Max and the girls again. I wanted to come back but not like this. Dotty has become so important to me, a close friend, a confidant, and a grandparent figure all rolled into one. I shake my head, trying to quell my anxiety, Dotty will be fine, she's such a trooper, so strong. I smile thinking about our first meeting and how my first impressions of her as a stern headteacher were a far cry from the soft, kind, funny person she really is. I pull the car over and Google the closest hospital; executing the perfect U-turn I head another half an hour out of town to find Dotty.

I walk into the hospital, furiously messaging Max and Joe. They don't respond, of course hospitals can be funny about phones. Max and I are barely even seeing each other but I can't fight the feeling this could be something special. That kiss was everything. A small part of me thinks perhaps he feels the same too. The trepidation after all my failed relationships hits me, but Max is different, perhaps it's being a dad or losing his wife, but I can tell he wouldn't do that. He's not a cheat.

I finally locate the ward Dotty is on. A tired looking nurse tells me it's outside of visiting hours and reminds me that it should *only* be family visiting right now and that if family says it's okay, I may be able to visit later. I feel foolish and self-conscious, what am I doing? I'm not family. I offer a big smile to hide my embarrassment and go back to my car to drive back to Dotty's, perhaps Max is there.

When I arrive at Dotty's the house is locked up, although Max's car is there. They must have gone out, maybe to the seaside as there's not much else in walking distance. I try his phone again. It's switched off. I decide to walk down to the coast anyway, it'll help clear my mind after the last few days and allow me to reflect on some of the things that have happened.

An ominous black cloud draws in and when I get down onto the beach there is hardly anyone about. There's a thickness in the air and the humidity is building so that you know the heavens could open at any moment. I sit on the beach in the same place

I bumped into Max before and look out over the sea. I watch a family play in the waves; three adult figures and two small children. As I watch they begin to walk back up the beach. Presumably deciding the cloud is too much of a threat. From here I can't tell if the two small figures are boys or girls but they remind me of Max, Joe and the girls and a tingle of happiness spreads through my body. I really have it bad for him now. There's still so much to tell Max and I wonder how he will take it, but I'm ready.

As I watch the family heading back up, I squint, really focusing on them. If I didn't know better, I would think that it was Max, Joe and the girls. The man even has a similar walk to Max. I hadn't even realised I knew how he walked, and I can see a thick head of hair. Come on, Anna, lots of people have thick hair and walk like that, I'm sure. I chide myself; I'm infatuated.

Finally, they are close enough that I can just about hear the shouts of the two children.

'Nene dance.' I hear it loud as I watch the smallest figure dance around and I know. It's them, they're here. But who are they with? I steel myself. Stop jumping to conclusions, just because of my bad experiences in the past I shouldn't let it ruin everything we have, that would be silly. It's probably a friend, maybe one of Joe's friends. They did grow up around here after all. I take a deep breath and stand up, ready to greet them. I feel a flush and the heat of my cheeks makes me wonder what I'm doing. He knows I care about Dotty. I'm here for Dotty but I know that's not the only reason. I feel suddenly nervous, is it just me? No, that kiss was not just me.

Max catches my eye as he gets closer, doing a double take as he registers who I am. Hazel spots me too and runs over to say hello. The woman he's with is a little behind Max with Neve's hand in hers, Neve begins to pull the woman towards me too. Joe is further back hurrying up the beach to catch up.

'Anna,' Max says, a soft frown forming on his face. 'You're here.' His words are flat and cold.

'Yes,' I say, with more conviction than I feel as I watch him look around at the woman. There's a moment of uncomfortable silence that falls between us all.

'Anna,' shouts Hazel, putting her arms around my legs and squeezing tight, oblivious to the tense atmosphere.

'Anna,' I hear Neve's little voice say as she gets closer and releases the woman's hand so she can wrap her little body around mine.

The woman has long dark, wavy hair and green eyes. She looks stunning in ripped jeans and a white t-shirt. Even Eloise would be jealous of her and *she* rarely sees other women as threats. This woman would be a threat. She gives me a tight smile, clearly uncomfortable. Everything is halted again, whilst Max, the woman and I look between each other. Puzzlement draws my eyebrows together as something begins to niggle and dawn on me. Perhaps I was wrong about Max after all.

'Mummy,' Hazel's voice cuts into my thoughts, as she takes hold of the brunette stunner's hand. 'Do you know Anna?'

'Mummy?' I choke out, looking for the answers in Max's face.

'Yes, hello, I'm Frances.' She smiles at me. The mother of Neve and Hazel holds out her hand to mine.

'But you said, b..but, b..but,' I stammer my words out, not wishing to spit it out in front of the children, trying to maintain any final shreds of dignity I might have left. I look to Joe as he arrives but there's a coldness there too.

Max's eyes are hard. 'We have things to discuss later.' Joe nods in agreement. Max looks positively furious. Why's Max angry? Upset he has been found out? Doesn't want me to reveal the kiss to his wife? Not wanting a scene. As if to answer my questions he indicates the children, silencing me. I look to Joe for reassurance, but he won't meet my eyes. He must have known all along, but he didn't know about Max and me.

I want to say she looks very much alive, that they lied to me but I don't. Instead, I give Hazel and Neve a big hug and Frances a nice smile, placing my hand in hers to greet her properly and pretend that my heart is not breaking all over again. I don't know who to feel worse for; me or his wife. Another cheat to add to the pile.

My chest is heavy as I walk up the beach, the disappointment is crushing.

I get back to the car and drive over to the hospital. I need to see Dotty even if it's over before it even began with Max. I check online about visiting hours and wait there until I can go in and see her. I sit and brood in the car, acting like a sulky teen until it's finally time. What now? Where do I go from here? I slump over the steering wheel and cry. Big sobs for all the things I've lost and what I thought I'd found. I could really do with seeing Dotty right now, a cup of her miracle tea would certainly help.

Finally, it's time. I go into the hospital and find the toilets first, cleaning up my face and trying to hide that I've been crying. I don't want Dotty to know, it's not her fault. Although I am concerned about her so hopefully, she won't guess it's for another reason. I just can't make sense of it. I feel betrayed. I just want to see she's okay for myself and say goodbye to my friend. Then I can go home.

Once on the ward, I pretend to be family to a friendly wide-eyed nurse who shows me straight to Dotty's room and there *he* is along with Joe. Dotty spots me before I have a chance to run and gives me a frail wave.

I enter the room, not wanting to cause a scene and genuinely wanting her to know I care.

'Hello, Dotty, how're you?' I ask, my voice sunny and bright.

'Been better dear,' she croaks, her voice small.

'Do you mind if I have a word with Anna, Gran?' Max's tone has changed back to the formal voice I remember from when we first met, back to when we were strangers.

She doesn't answer but bats us away with her hand, Joe stays with Dotty, sitting at her side and sharing one of their private jokes.

We go into the hallway and I'm preparing myself for the usual excuses. The reasons it's okay that he cheats, the begging not to reveal his betrayal to his wife. But they don't come, instead I'm met with a steely stare and knotted brows. It's as though he's mad at me. The heat and anger begin to rise in my chest.

I wait for him to speak and finally through gritted teeth he says, 'The hospital seems to think Gran hasn't been taking all of her medication, but I said she has a carer so I'm really confused. Has she been taking her meds?'

I step back at the venom of the last sentence. Her meds? I think back over the time that I've been staying with her, the white lie about being her carer; I'd almost forgotten about it. Now isn't the time to rat Dotty out and anyway I'm mad at him too. I remember her taking some pills some mornings, but I couldn't say if she did it every morning. The guilt engulfs me, I was staying in her home; I could have kept an eye on her. Not that Dotty would have welcomed it but I should have looked after her more, instead, she looked after me.

'Yes, I think so,' I stammer, unsure of myself.

'You think so?' he growls.

'That's what I said,' I raise my voice to match his, refusing to be intimidated.

'What kind of carer are you?' he accuses.

I feel sick that I hadn't been looking after Dotty, even though I'm not the carer he thinks I am, but I am still her friend.

I ignore him instead. 'Is Dotty going to be okay?'

'Yes, no thanks to you. And you're sacked. I'm going to pop down to the gift shop now so say goodbye and leave. Who were you employed by again? I'll be having words.' He's furious and all I can do is stare. There are no words and I understand why he's so upset but it doesn't stop me from being cross with him too.

'Dotty has my info,' I say, not wanting to perpetrate the lie any further but not able to out my friend.

I go back into the room to see Dotty. Everything is such a mess and I'm still furious with him. Joe gets up to give us some space and I can feel he's not too pleased with me either.

'I'll be back in a bit, Gran,' he speaks softly and his eyes quickly dart to me before he leaves the room without another word.

'Hello, Anna.' Her voice comes out small but there's a smile in it.

'Hello.' I attempt to move the corners of my mouth up too, but it comes out a little watery.

'Oh dear, what's happened?' There's no hiding it from Dotty even in her current state.

I shrug.

'It's not that grandson of mine, is it?'

I nod, silent and afraid the slightest sound will make me start crying.

'Is he cross about the carer thing?' she asks, sharp as ever.

I clear my throat willing it to come out clearly. 'He thinks I'm not a good carer and that you haven't been taking your medication?'

'Oh no! I'm so sorry; this is all my fault. He's blaming you all because of that little lie I told. He's a stubborn man but a good one, I'll explain it all to him and everything will be okay.' She pats my hand reassuringly and I feel awful that she's comforting me. A rogue tear escapes. 'Don't worry Anna, we can clear this all up.'

'It's not that.' I wobble. 'I just met his wife. I didn't… I hadn't... I just feel stupid, you know.' I think back to the kiss. His poor wife, although why she wasn't down before, but she's obviously come down now, when something horrible has happened. She probably has no idea.

'Frances?' she asks, looking puzzled.

'He doesn't have more wives, does he?'

'Well, no, but she's his ex-wife.'

'Really?'

'Yes, been separated for a few years and divorced for probably a year and a half or so. They're working on co-parenting, for the kids.' Dotty looks awkward. 'It's really not my story to tell. I think you and Max need to have a proper conversation and get everything out in the open. You have my permission to tell him about not being my carer. I'm sorry I've put you in that position, but even an old lady can see there's a spark between you.' There's a familiar twinkle in her eye and I thought I'd hidden it so well from her. 'You may have something special, and it's worth exploring without misinformation. Please go and talk to him.'

My cheeks redden as I realise there's no getting anything past Dotty.

'I thought she was dead?' I finally manage, holding on to the one piece of information I had on his wife, isn't that what he said, and Joe.

'Who told you that?' she queries.

I think back to when it all came to light. 'I overheard you and Max talking,' I admit.

'You must have heard something wrong, it's very complicated. I really don't think I'm the one to tell you about it.'

'But he confirmed it too.' Didn't he?

Chapter 26

I don't have to wait long before Max is back, poking his head around the door; his face grim when he sees me.

'I think you two need to talk,' Dotty croaks. 'Now come on Max, don't blame Anna. She can explain.' She closes her eyes once she's finished her sentence, exhausted from the whole exchange, she looks older than she did before and grey-faced, so grey and small. I think about my grandparents and how they looked close to the end of their lives and I can't help but think how she doesn't look a million miles away from that. But Dotty's a fighter, she'll be fine. I know I was only saying I was her carer but how could I have been so naive and not give the help she clearly needed. She seemed so capable; age is just a number.

'Come on then.' Max ushers me out of the room, his mood hasn't lifted even with Dotty's promise of explanations. I don't try to make any small talk like I usually would, after all, I'm not the only one who should do some explaining.

We head outside the hospital and find a bench to sit on.

'I can't imagine what you have to say that's going to make me any less angry about the situation,' Max starts firmly. 'I hope you know I'm only speaking with you for Gran's sake.'

'I'm not Dotty's carer.'

'No shit Sherlock, definitely not anymore and I will be talking to your employer.'

'No, I mean, I never was.'

He sits up straighter, surprised by Dotty and mine's deception.

'Who are you then?' he spits.

'I'd had a bad day,' I say, dismissing and diminishing the worst wedding I've ever attended. 'I just wanted to get away so I drove to the beach and my car broke down and Dotty put me up.' It tumbles out of me as one long breathy sentence.

He sighs, still unimpressed, not ready to budge an inch.

'So, you're just on your holidays, taking advantage of an old woman's kind nature?'

'It wasn't like that,' I plead. 'And anyway, you should know all about taking advantage of people.' It slips out before I can stop myself and I see his eyebrows raise slightly which is the only tell he has taken my comment in at all. His posture remains rigid and straight, I think back then to the man I first met and the man I also know him to be, much softer, a good dad and kind.

'What's that supposed to mean?'

'Your wife is alive?' I accuse.

He draws back and stares at me. 'Yes, she's alive. And she's my ex-wife, it's been over for a while and I don't always feel the need to explain a very complicated situation to someone I've just met.'

I nod awkwardly but I still need to know. Our trust is broken and perhaps there are things I should tell him too.

I take a deep breath, ready to reveal the shame I've tried desperately to avoid and even with some of the resolution I've garnered from the last few days, it's still hard to tell someone new about the whole situation.

'The day I came down here, I had been to my best friend's wedding.'

A frown forms on his face as he tries to work out the relevance.

'She had been my best friend since we were children, we were practically sisters, always at each other's houses, always together. Anyway, I went to the wedding with my boyfriend, who then stood up during the ceremony and objected to the marriage because he was in love with *her*. My best friend. To say it was humiliating is an understatement and I did the only thing I could think at the time and that was to run.'

Max's mouth drops open and he puts his hand through his hair. I watch him try to take the information in.

'That must have been very hard,' he says evenly.

'Thank you, it was. We'd been together for five years and I thought he was my forever person, but

I've learnt so much over the last few weeks of being here. It turns out my best friend had been having an affair with my partner and I'd changed so much for both of them but over the last few weeks it's as though I found myself, I woke up and... I found you,' I add shyly at the end, looking up at him.

'So where does Dotty come into this?' he asks more softly.

'I drove down to the coast in his car, I couldn't find anywhere to stay and someone told me about Dotty's layby and so I went there. I couldn't get the roof closed and I got soaked and had a little sleep in the car and that's where Dotty found me. At probably my lowest point. She has been so kind to me and when you came, she told you I was her carer and I went along with it, and I'm sorry for that. I really thought this amazing woman was more than capable of looking after herself.'

'She is, but it's not to say she's not getting older and doesn't need help as much as she tries to pretend she doesn't.'

I nod, understanding Max's concerns more than ever now. I let out a big breath, it's a relief to get it all off my chest.

'I'm really sorry, I thought you were being overprotective and I should have understood your concerns more. I did help around the house and did the shopping but I didn't get involved with her meds.'

Max almost laughs. 'Gran never ceases to amaze me, I mean, granted when I saw you dressed...' He scans my face for a reaction as he says, 'rather bizarrely, I should have guessed really. Gran has a kind heart and you're not the first person she has brought home to look after. I'm glad you tried to help her too. I just wish I'd known so I could have asked her more about her meds. Fortunately, Gran is going to be okay.'

'I am really sorry, when Dotty suggested it I really couldn't see the harm,' I say solemnly, feeling tears spring to my eyes. What if Dotty hadn't been okay?

'It's okay, I should have guessed it was Gran's idea. I'm sorry I was so cross with you. Gran means so much to me and I think I took it all out on you. Everything has been very stressful since Frances came back into our lives.'

It's my turn to raise an eyebrow, back into their lives? I don't say anything though, giving him space to expand, mirroring my own parents' way.

'Frances and I were married but our marriage wasn't perfect; we had Hazel and everything was quite strained between us. To be honest I think we would have split up then but we found out she was pregnant with Neve. After Neve was born, I think Frances had some sort of mental breakdown, perhaps it was post-natal, perhaps it was all the reasons why we really should not have been together any longer. Then when Neve was six months old, she left us for another man. He was a neighbour of ours, it started as an emotional affair when she was pregnant and turned into more a few months after Neve was born. I tried to get her to come back, to see if she would get some help even if she didn't want us to be together anymore, but she decided she didn't want to see us or even have a relationship with the children. It's been incredibly hard on Hazel; the abandonment has affected her profusely and me.' He diverts his eyes. 'Neve is the luckier one as she doesn't really remember any different so the whole situation is better for her. It was so hard when she left me, her family weren't much help, and everyone seemed to blame me. We had a rough patch where communication broke down and I thought that my children would have no mum but recently Frances has been doing a lot of work on herself. Going to therapy and working through the mental issues she has and she's asked to be back in the children's lives. She lives down here and that's why we come down so much to visit, there's been a lot of mediation to sort out the arrangements and that's why I've been here and there.'

It's Max's turn to let out the deep sigh.

'Wow, you've been so understanding.' I try to imagine myself in Max's shoes.

'It was hard for the longest time to understand but there was so much going on. She shouldn't have cheated and for a while that really stuck with me but it was about so much more than that. We weren't right together and she was struggling with her mental health, the pregnancy hormones and possible post-natal depression pushed her over the edge. I'm glad she is trying to have a relationship with the girls again, it's nice to see her in a better place and I hope that we can undo some of the pain that was caused, particularly to Hazel.'

The huge guard that Max has had up since the

start makes sense now, his protectiveness, his manner, they all fall into place. This is a guy who's been hurt but who has made the best of what happened.

'Thank you for telling me.' I feel humbled by his sharing something so painful. I don't know why we both kept everything so close to our own hearts. Max is more similar to me than I had realised.

We sit in silence for a moment reflecting on the magnitude of what we have both just shared and how much closer it has brought us.

I look down at our hands and Max's is entwined in mine.

Chapter 27

Christmas

'What time are they getting here?' Hazel hops from foot to foot; she's excited and maybe a little nervous but what's not to love about her?

'Any minute now, sweetie.'

I take her tiny hand in mine, and we finish setting the table together, arranging the crackers perfectly.

There's a loud knock on the door and I know who it is already from the signature sound. I pull the door open to see my parents standing there, grinning from ear to ear and laden with Christmas presents. I've been more or less living between their home, here and Max's place in London, but this is the first time I've brought all the people I love together. There's a nervous anticipation in the air, please let it go well. How could it not?

'Merry Christmas.' They both grin and there is a softness and calmness that resonates from them that I've come to really appreciate. Before I always wanted the busy, chaotic family of Eloise. I've come to realise that sometimes the grass is not greener on the other side. I bring them both into an embrace and spot Mum shyly waving at Hazel who is hiding behind the doorway. My parents have heard so much about these two little girls, Mum says it feels as if she already knows them.

Neve runs up to the doorway straight away.

'Hello, merry kissmas,' she says in a small voice, smiling sweetly. She'll have them eating out of the palm of her hand in no time, just like everyone else.

Hazel is still watching from further away, she's not ready to come and say hello yet but she'll get there. I watch as Neve goes over to her and they hold hands and she brings her sister over towards my parents.

'Do you want to come and meet my mum and dad,' I ask softly.

Hazel allows Neve to lead her through, her voice lost, which is so unlike Hazel it almost shocks me. I think about everything she has been through with Frances, so much for someone so small.

We've been preparing the dinner all day, under instruction from Dotty but I've incorporated some things I've learnt. My cooking has certainly become better since I tried before. Dotty is doing well and between us and a real carer who pops in every morning we have her medications handled. Dotty didn't like it at first, but she's come around to it now and she actually gets on really well with Tina.

Another knock at the door and the girls are up again; it's all go today. I pull the door open to find Frances standing a little awkwardly on the doorstep.

I smile; she smiles and we exchange Merry Christmases. We've all come a long way since that day on the beach and I think we're kind of friends now, or at least friendly. She's agreed to come for lunch so the girls can have their first Christmas with everyone together. The girls are thrilled to have Mummy around and their relationship is really coming along, which has had a really good impact on Hazel especially.

Max comes and greets Frances warmly, so it's only Joe to come now and we'll be a full house. A final rat-a-tat-tat on the door and Dotty goes through excitedly to answer with me and the girls following close behind. When we pull the door open, Joe is standing there, but he's not alone. Beside him is a handsome gentleman a little shorter than Joe. with jet black hair and green eyes. He's all smiles and Joe looks at him sheepishly.

'Is there room for one more,' he asks, reaching his hand out to the handsome stranger.

'Of course!' Dotty calls, pulling Joe in for a reassuring hug. 'And who might this handsome man be? Your boyfriend?' she asks and you can see the air deflate from Joe, he doesn't need to say it. She already knows, I think back to her saying I'm not Joe's type and it dawns on me she probably knew all along.

'Yes, Gran he is, this is Caleb.'

'Nice to meet you.' He reaches out his hand but instead he's engulfed in a massive Dotty hug. I look over Dotty's head at Joe who is beaming now. Caleb is the first boyfriend he has wanted to bring to meet everyone. I've met him a few times in London and I even suggested he bring him but he'd been so unsure I thought he might not be ready yet. I think Dotty has surprised him; she really doesn't care as long as he is happy. I knew it would be fine.

Joe comes and gives me a kiss on the cheek before going through into the living room to greet the other guests and cuddle the girls. I go around the room, making sure everyone is comfortable and has a drink in hand before we all settle into the living room. The fire is on and Dotty opted for a real tree this year, saying you need it when you have guests. It looks beautiful, we've had to get people to bring chairs down so we can all fit in but we've done it, it's snug but so nice to all be together. I look around at everyone I love and I'm so humbled and happy.

Hazel tugs at my arm as I take my seat. 'Yes, sweetie?' I ask.

'Can I open presents now?' She puts her little hands together in a praying position and Neve copies her.

'Pease, Anna?' Neve echoes, batting her eyes at me.

They both look over at Frances. 'Can we Mummy?' they plead.

'Dinner's almost ready so I think we should do them afterwards.' She smiles.

'I have got a little something from me they could have now if that's okay?' I check with Frances, and she nods happily. She's doing really well now, continuing her therapy and her relationship with the girls has really come along, the change in Hazel has been enormous.

They jump up and down eagerly as I hand them something special I've made for them. They rip off the wrapping paper to find matching cardigans, which I've worked really hard to crochet. I've also created a tiny teddy each that fits inside the pockets. I point towards it and their little faces light up as they take out the tiny teddies. Neve cuddles hers and they both throw their arms around me. 'Thank you.'

'Wow, Anna, those are lovely,' Mum appraises, inspecting Hazel's cardigan.

I'm really proud of them, I've used a really soft purple wool and added some big buttons for effect. The teddies are made of the same wool with tiny buttons for eyes and a stitched mouth.

'How's it going, selling at the markets?' Dad asks.

'It's going really well; the clothes and the soft toys seem to sell the best and are the quickest for me to crochet. Although I do love making the big blankets too.'

I've set up an *Etsy* and recently started selling at a local Sunday market. The nest egg that Mum and Dad gave me has really helped me to start it all up and get the wool I needed. I'm nearly breaking even now and I'm hoping next year I'll be making a profit.

'Yes, she's very talented.' Max grins, holding up his glass.

'She certainly is,' Dotty agrees.

I smile at everyone, so grateful for them all.

'Did you meet up with Jane the other day?' Mum asks.

'Yes, she filled me in on all the gossip from the

hotel.'

'Oh, yes?' Joe asks, ever one to enjoy a bit of gossip.

I filled Joe in on everything that had happened and the pretending to be Dotty's carer after Max, and he took it all very well, he found it hilarious and typical Dotty.

'Eddie and Eloise have officially split, divorce pending, apparently Eloise is dating one of the managers at the hotel now.'

'She always manages to land on her feet.' Mum rolls her eyes.

'Yes, she does, I don't wish anything bad for her though. We may no longer be friends and I hate what she did, but she has lost Eddie through this. It can't have been easy.'

'You're a far kinder person than me,' Joe scoffs. 'If someone had done that to me, I would be wishing horrible things for them.'

Caleb's eyebrows shoot up and we all laugh.

'Have you heard anything of Will?'

'No and I'm not interested, in a funny sort of way I'm grateful it all happened.'

'Really?' Max questions.

'Well, if he hadn't been a cheat I'd never have driven down here and my life would be quite different. And now I've met someone pretty special,' I say, my cheeks colouring as I look over at Max. 'I'm doing something I really enjoy, and I've made some amazing friends.' I look over at Dotty. It really has been an amazing journey; I may not have enjoyed all of it but it has got me here. Where I'm meant to be.

After I sorted everything out with Max, we finally admitted to ourselves and everyone else there was something there. We took it slow for us and the kids, but it's been going really well and we're so happy in each other's company. Max is a kind and loving man and although he has his grumpy moments, I really love him.

Joe raises his glass, grinning at all of us.

'To all the cheats,' he says, and we all laugh.

THE END

Amelia Watchman

L♥ve, HATE and Indifference

She's on the road trip of her life to find closure - what could possibly go wrong?

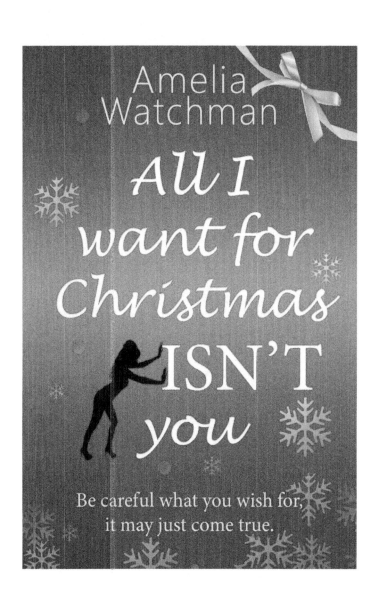

Amelia
Watchman

All I
want for
Christmas
ISN'T
you

Be careful what you wish for,
it may just come true.

Amelia Watchman

It's all
about
me,
maybe

You can't always get what you want,
but you may just get what you need

Printed in Great Britain
by Amazon

45138427R00118